Praise for *Ke...*

"This sparkling combination... ... ... magic is
bound to enchant."
—*Kirkus Reviews*

"Excellent. . . . The writing is refreshingly well
done and weaves together the author's knowledge of
art, folklore, and botany to paint a magical world where
readers' senses are piqued by the likes of stone fairies,
cave anemones, and a queen named Patchouli."
—*SLJ*

"Great for girls who love fairies and magical worlds."
—KidzWorld.com

Praise for *Birdie's Book*

"Bozarth's tale is a beguiling mix of magic, adventure
and eco-awareness, and her message of girl-power and
positive change will resonate with tween readers."
—*Kirkus Reviews*

"A fun, light read that ought to be a hit with girls who
like adventure and magic."
—Books for Kids (blog)

"Bozarth has taken the best aspects of various young
adult genres and mixed them together in a fresh and
optimistic way."
—Kidsreads.com

The Fairy Godmother Academy

The Fairy Godmother Academy

Book 6

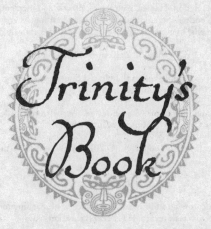

Trinity's Book

Jan Bozarth

A YEARLING BOOK

Copyright © 2013 by FGA Media Inc.

All rights reserved. Published in the United States by Yearling, an imprint of Random House Children's Books, a division of Random House, Inc., New York.

Yearling and the jumping horse design are registered trademarks of Random House, Inc.

"Learn to Fly" copyright © 2012 by Blue Arrow Music

Visit us on the Web!
randomhouse.com/kids

Educators and librarians, for a variety of teaching tools,
visit us at RHTeachersLibrarians.com

Visit FairyGodmotherAcademy.com

Library of Congress Cataloging-in-Publication Data
Bozarth, Jan.
Trinity's book / Jan Bozarth. — 1st ed.
p. cm. — (The Fairy Godmother Academy ; bk. 6)
Summary: "Trinity travels to Aventurine and discovers her gift of flight."—
Provided by publisher.
ISBN 978-0-375-86576-3 (pbk.) — ISBN 978-0-375-89606-4 (ebook)
[1. Fairy godmothers—Fiction. 2. Fairies—Fiction. 3. Magic—Fiction. 4. Flight—
Fiction. 5. Babies—Fiction. 6. Adventure and adventurers—Fiction.] I. Title.
PZ7.B6974Tri 2012 [Fic]—dc23 2012021268

Printed in the United States of America
10 9 8 7 6 5 4 3 2 1

First Yearling Edition 2013

*To all the girls and women taking
risks, growing, and moving toward
their dreams. "Learn to Fly" is
our anthem!*

Contents

1

Kites

It felt strange to be celebrating the Maori New Year on a beautiful spring day in New York City. In New Zealand, half a world away, my friends and family were also celebrating, but it was autumn.

I could imagine leaves falling from the trees in Auckland, and a chill in the morning air. But carrying my kite into Central Park, I could see that it was sparkling green with new growth, and the day was T-shirt warm. Only the breeze was just right.

"This looks like a good spot," my father said. He set the picnic basket on the ground near a large sturdy oak and slipped off his kite bag.

I looked at the tree and smiled. *Just begging to be climbed,* I thought.

"Good on you, Henry Jones!" My mother's bronze face glowed with the warmth of her smile. "It's an excellent choice. There's shade and lots of grass."

"I'm so glad you approve, Marissa," my father teased.

I laughed. "Dad, you're such a hard case."

"Watch the Kiwi, Trinity," said my father with a wink.

Oops! I had to be careful about using my Kiwi—or New Zealand—expressions here in the States. "Hard case" meant an amusing person in New Zealand. In America, it meant someone who was rough and stubborn. Not my dad at all.

My Maori mother had called my American father by both his first and last names for as long as I could remember. He just called her Marissa. Sometimes he added, "The light of my life." He had fallen in love with her fourteen years ago, when he first arrived in New Zealand to photograph the *Matariki* kites for a travel magazine. My mother had loved him at first sight, too. They married and had me a year later.

"Right here?" Dad asked, shaking out a large blanket.

Mom scanned the ground, squinting with a critical eye. "I don't see any rocks," she said. Then she grinned and grabbed two corners of the blanket to help lay it flat. "It'll do just fine."

"Thank the stars," my father said, pretending to be greatly relieved. "I'm hungry!"

"We'll eat as soon as everything is set out," Mom said.

"Do you need help?" I asked.

"No, Trinity," Dad answered. "Have a look around, but don't go too far. We'll call when we're ready."

I found a safe spot for my kite and rushed toward the huge oak. Quickly moving from one large branch to another, soon I was about twenty feet off the ground. From my vantage point in the tree, I could see the grassy field where we would fly our kites after lunch. Several kids were already there, flying kites they had bought in stores. Brightly colored paper and plastic diamonds, dragons, birds, and superheroes bobbed, dove, and fluttered against the clear blue sky. The little ones cried when they crashed or got caught in a tree.

That happened a lot. Although American kids seemed to share the Maori joy of kite flying, they sent their kites into the sky to soar or die on the whims of the wind. They had no control, and when their fragile birds broke, they threw away the pieces.

A Maori would never treat a kite in such a disrespectful manner. But of course, a Maori kite was not one of millions produced by machines. Each was unique, made by the hands that flew it, and most could be repaired. If not, it was either kept or buried and returned to the earth with reverence.

They aren't toys, I thought.

Historically, Maori kites were much more than sources of amusement. Some were fashioned and flown in rituals. Others had been designed to carry warriors over the walls of enemy encampments. Huge kites built to cut through clouds were tethered with long ropes held by many men.

At least, that's how it had been before the Europeans came in the 1800s. *Aotearoa,* the Maori word for "New Zealand," had been quickly transformed. All the ancient kites were destroyed or lost, and the colorful expressions of our Maori culture were absent from our skies until *manu tukutuku,* the ancient art of kite craft, was brought back in the 1970s.

My mother taught me how to make a traditional tailless kite from grass, bark, and flax.

The love of flying it was in my Maori blood.

Unlike my ancestors, I did not believe that kites were mystical objects that connected heaven and earth, but sometimes I felt like *I* could fly. The feeling always hit me hard when I stood a thousand feet in the air on the Sky Tower in Auckland. I even felt it now, a few feet off the ground in a tree.

Just spread your arms wide and let yourself go, the tree seemed to be telling me.

I came to my senses before I went splat on the

ground. It was just a silly dream—childish. People could not fly.

"Come and get it!" Dad yelled.

I answered as I always do, "Get what?"

"Nothing if I eat it all first!" Dad joked with a booming laugh. Then, as he took a container of puff pastry squares out of the basket, he looked at Mom and faked a frown. "Next time we're going to a park that lets people grill real picnic food."

"Whatever you want, Henry Jones," Mom said.

"I want hot dogs, hamburgers, potato salad, pickles, and chips." He laughed again and kissed Mom on the cheek.

I wanted to go back to New Zealand. I missed the seaside city of Auckland. We had lived there until just after I turned twelve, almost a year ago. When my mother took a job as a commercial pilot based out of LaGuardia airport, we had to move to New York.

Dad was a freelance photographer who traveled on assignment. It didn't matter if he flew out of Auckland or New York, so he didn't mind where we lived.

I minded a lot! I didn't want to leave my life and friends, especially Holly Jackson. We've been as close as sisters since we were three. At birth, she was named Hakeke, the Maori word for "mountain holly," but I've always called her Holly. So does everyone else.

I sat cross-legged on the blanket and heaped a paper plate with Maori feast food. I loved beef wrapped in banana leaves, which Mom had found at a specialty food store. The aroma of spiced meat was tantalizing, even though it hadn't been cooked in an *umu*, pits dug into the earth back in New Zealand. Mom had to use a slow cooker in our apartment kitchen. The tuna salad was tart and the bread melted in my mouth, but I did not take any of the traditional roasted sweet potatoes that most Maori loved. I hated *kumara*!

"Don't eat too much, Trinity," Dad warned. "You won't be able to keep up with your kite."

"My *manu* won't get away from me," I said.

"How many friends are coming to your slumber party tomorrow?" my mother asked.

"Three," I said. "That's all I invited."

Life in the United States had gone from homesick to tolerable to practically glorious the instant I had enrolled in the Girls' International School of Manhattan. There I met my new friends, Sumi, Zally, and Lilu.

"I still have to shop," my mother muttered as she reached for a container of berries. "And I'll need a list. Popcorn, fizzy drinks, cake . . ."

"Cake!" Dad stood up and pulled Mom away

from the basket. "Let's save dessert for later and go fly a kite!"

Mom looked at me sideways, and we both smiled. My dad was very much an artist. I'd inherited my mom's love of numbers and logic, and our methodical, practical way of getting through life often mystified him.

But he understood our deep bond with the kites, and he embraced the art of *manu tuku-tuku* as though it were part of his own heritage. Taking pictures of kites had brought my mom and dad together.

We took the kites out of our bags and held them high off the ground as we headed to the field. Mine resembled a bird with a pointed head, an elongated tail, and stubby wings. In keeping with the old ways, our *manu* were decorated with natural fibers and dyes, feathers, shells, and flowers. I had cheated and used colored ribbons laced through the reeds to secure several seashells. The colors brightened the brown of the dry grasses, and my heart swelled with pride when I looked at it.

"When do you leave for Florida?" Mom asked. Dad had been hired by an entertainment magazine to do a photo layout of wildlife tourist attractions in Orlando.

"Two weeks," he answered.

I fell back a step to let them talk in private. I had other things on my mind, mostly the awesome fact that I would turn thirteen tomorrow, and I was going to share my birthday with my closest friends.

All except Holly, who was eight thousand miles away.

I pulled my phone out of my pocket and sent her a text: *Skype! 3:00 p.m. Sunday your time!*

If I still lived in Auckland, it would already be my birthday.

But I wouldn't know Sumi, Zally, and Lilu.

I grinned, thinking about my friends. We weren't alike at all, and yet somehow we worked.

On my first day at the Girls' International School of Manhattan, Zally gave me a giant chocolate chip cookie from her family's bakery. Her infectious grin and bubbly good humor made me feel instantly welcome and at ease, and we quickly became friends. As a math lover, I could totally relate to the detailed precision of her fabulous maps. But I *didn't* understand why she put so much thought and energy into charts of make-believe places.

I met Sumi and Lilu in algebra.

Sumi, an aspiring fashion designer who sees something beautiful in everything, and Lilu, an accomplished weaver who blushes at praise, were totally befuddled by that day's lesson. I gave them some tips on how to solve the equations. Lilu gave me one of her friendship bracelets.

Sumi noticed my rough, calloused hands and told me they were a thousand times more beautiful than ones that never worked or made anything. I told her all about my passion for climbing rock walls, which is how I got the calluses.

"We should put some space between us and the other fliers," Dad said. "Their puny little kites are seriously outmatched by our monster *manu*!"

"You're not worried about some child's kite, Henry Jones," Mom said. "You just don't want to be taking time to answer questions."

"You're right," he said. "You answer them!"

I laughed as my father started running. His kite was airborne in seconds, slicing through the sky like a hawk tethered to his hand by twine.

A few seconds later, three boys showed up. Mom left to join Dad, leaving me to handle the questions. Someone always asked about our strange kites when we flew them.

"Is that a kite?" A redheaded boy with freckles pointed at my kite. "Where'd you get it?"

"It *is* a kite, and I made it," I said.

"No, you didn't," a short boy with a buzz cut scoffed.

I held his gaze in chilly silence. It didn't matter if he was being mean or showing off. He had called me a liar.

"I bet she did, Jordan," the third boy said. He was cute with a mop of curly dark hair and brown eyes. "I saw pictures of kites like that in my geography book. From Australia, I think."

"New Zealand," I said.

"See," Freckles teased in a snide voice. "You don't know everything, Parker."

"Never said I did," Parker shot back.

"It won't fly," Jordan said.

I bit my tongue.

"Those two are flying." Parker shielded his eyes from the sun and pointed at my parents' kites.

Jordan shrugged. "Who cares about kites anyway? They're not good for anything."

"Maori warriors rode kites and swooped down on their enemies," I said calmly. "With spears."

"Awesome!" Parker exclaimed.

Jordan rolled his eyes.

"Get real!" Freckles laughed. "That kite couldn't carry a chipmunk."

I *never* have the patience to deal with boys who think they're so smart and so cool that they can be totally obnoxious and nobody will care. I ran down the rise and launched my kite into the sky.

"Hey!" Parker shouted. "Do you come here a lot?"

I pretended I didn't hear. Parker seemed like an okay guy. I hadn't talked to him long enough to be sure. But I absolutely could not *stand* his friends.

I walked toward Mom and Dad, slowly letting the line out until my ribbon-feathered bird was almost as high as theirs.

"I hope you were nice," Mom said.

"I wasn't mean," I said.

"That's good," my father said absently. He winced when a gust caught his *manu* and pitched it to the side. The kite seemed doomed to fall, but he worked the twine, pulling it in and letting it out until the kite stabilized.

"That was close," I said.

"Too close," Dad agreed. "Still, I think I'm finally getting the hang of this. Want to see a loop-the-loop?"

"Like this?" Mom twisted and snapped her wrist. The flat grasses in her kite whistled and rattled as the triangle swooped through the air in a wide arc.

"Or this." Dad yanked his line. Instead of zipping around in a tight circle, his kite shook and struggled to stay aloft.

"Here!" Mom handed me her line and grabbed Dad's. An expert kite flier since she was a girl, my mother had an incredible sense of air currents and twine. She quickly brought the kite under control and gave it back to my father.

"*Ta.*" He used the New Zealand word for "thanks," then smiled and kissed her. "No more fancy stuff today."

Dad wasn't a natural like my mother and me, but he didn't usually have so much trouble. Then I realized that we had forgotten something vital.

"I know what's wrong." I began to chant the family's *turu manu,* a kite charm that would make the kites fly better. Mom and Dad joined in.

The practice of singing as the kites ascended was as old as kites, and most Maori knew the ancient ritual chants that had been handed down through the generations. We always sang the lines my grandmother had composed for my mother years and years ago.

My bird is a beauty flier.
My bird is a golden hawk.

My bird reaches for the stars,
To fly beyond forever.

As we recited the words over and over, our three kites climbed steadily higher. Many modern Maori still believed that chanting had some mysterious mystical effect on kites, but that was just a silly superstition. The kites flew better because the repetition and cadence of chanting calmed and strengthened the *people* who were flying the kites.

I didn't try to explain that anymore. My friends back in New Zealand didn't care why it worked as long as it worked.

Half an hour later, we called it quits for the day.

"Now it's time for dessert." Dad patted his stomach as we walked back to our picnic spot.

"Sugar berries," I said. "Yum."

"I think they'll taste a lot better with pound cake fresh from Alma de Chocolate," Dad said. "Don't you?"

"Absolutely!" I exclaimed. Alma de Chocolate was Zally's family bakery. "They make the best pound cake in the world!"

"I'll be right back," Dad said as he ran ahead.

Mom smiled slightly and shook her head. "It's almost like he knows."

"Knows what?" I asked.

"That you and I need time alone to talk."

My thoughts raced as I followed Mom back to our picnic spot. When parents wanted to talk, it was almost always about something bad or embarrassing.

What was so important it had to ruin our wonderful day?

2

Tall Tales

"I've got an early birthday present for you," Mom said as she put her kite away.

"What is it?" I asked, trying to keep the relief out of my voice. I stowed my kite and joined her on the blanket. I felt guilty for assuming the worst.

"Something I hope you'll treasure as much as I do." She pulled a velvet box out of the picnic basket and handed it to me.

I took the box, but I didn't open it. Mom's tone and the serious look in her eyes were clues: The gift was important somehow.

"Open it," Mom urged.

I lifted the lid, saw the familiar greenstone beads, and gasped. "This is *your* necklace!"

"It's yours now." Mom smiled, mistaking my dismay as delight. "By tradition, the necklace is passed on when a daughter turns thirteen."

The jade necklace with the round, silver-dollar-sized pendant had been in our family for generations. I cherished my Ananya heritage, but I did not believe the lineage talisman was a source of mystical power. My mother did. That's why she always wore it.

Until now, I thought. I hadn't noticed it was missing because Mom didn't always wear it outside her clothes. Today, I had assumed the pendant was under her T-shirt. I had been too excited about flying kites to pay closer attention.

"Thanks, Mom." I held the pendant in my hand and traced the etched Maori tattoo with my finger. The design was the ancient symbol for the family name. "I don't know what to say."

"That's all right," Mom said. "I have a lot to tell you. For one thing, this is much more than just a beautiful piece of jewelry."

"What is it?" I asked, intrigued.

"It's magical," Mom said with a wistful smile.

I did not roll my eyes, but it was an effort.

Mom took the necklace from my hand and depressed a thumbnail clasp. The top of the pendant opened like an old-fashioned pocket watch.

"It opens!" I exclaimed, stunned.

My mom had worn the necklace all my life, and I never knew it had a hidden compartment. I felt stung.

Then I realized that revealing the secret was probably something saved for when daughters were given the necklace.

I stared at the pendant, fascinated by the miniature technology inside. A transparent crystal covered an intricate mechanism of colorful ultrafine filaments intermeshed with delicate cogs and gears. The movement was so silent and flawless the device *did* seem more magical than mechanical.

"What does it do?" I asked.

"The compass calculates everything you'll need to know when you learn to fly," Mom said. "Wind, weather, direction, cloud conditions . . ."

Mom's incredible words were spoken so matter-of-factly I wasn't sure I had heard her correctly.

"Like this." Mom held the open compass in the palm of her hand and spoke into it. "Wind."

The image of a yellow daffodil appeared on the crystal. The bloom bobbed and the stem bent slightly to depict a gentle breeze. After a few seconds, the flower faded away.

I was too stuck on my mother's previous announcement to be amazed by the hologram.

"Fly?" I asked. Then, suddenly realizing she could only mean one thing, I gasped again. This time my delight was real. "Are you and Dad giving me flying lessons for my birthday?"

"Flying airplanes?" Mom looked startled. "No, that's not . . ."

I was disappointed but not surprised. I badgered my parents on a regular basis about learning to pilot a small plane, but their argument was always the same: I was too young.

"Hang gliding!" I exclaimed. I often imagined what it would be like to plunge off a cliff harnessed to a delta-wing sail. In my dreams, I knew instinctively how to steer and take advantage of the air currents. A hang glider was the closest a modern Maori could come to riding a kite like the ancients.

"No, Trinity," Mom said with a hint of exasperation. "Just listen for a minute and I'll explain."

"Okay." I sighed and sat back on my heels.

Mom paused to take a deep breath before she began. "As you know, the women in the Ananya Lineage all have certain traits in common. An innate love of flying is just one of them."

"The best one," I said, bracing myself for the outrageous and totally unbelievable parts that came next.

Normally, I had no patience for Mom's wild stories about family ties to an imaginary land where girls trained to be fairy godmothers. She always spoke as though the tales were true and shrugged when I insisted it was all nonsense. My friends at the new school believed eerily similar stories about their families. It was exasperating, but I never accused them of being naïve and gullible *drongo*. I would never call my mother an idiot, either. I just nodded and tried to look interested.

"But it's more than just a love of flying," Mom went on. She closed the pendant and gave it back to me. "It's a gift. When we truly believe we can fly, we can."

I almost laughed but choked it back. The idea was preposterous, but I couldn't deny that if I could have one impossible wish, it would be to fly. I was also oddly comforted knowing that I shared this with my mom, and my grandmother before her.

"But you have to believe to the very core of your being and know that it's true," Mom said. "Otherwise you'll be grounded with no hope of ever breaking free."

It made no sense; my mother's degrees in engineering and hours of training in the cockpit had turned her dream of flying into a reality, but for some reason she thought that something magical in her blood and not hard work had made it possible. When my mom talked like this, I always looked for a way to end the conversation quickly.

"I believe I can do anything I set my mind to, Mom." I smiled to reassure her. "You and Dad taught me that."

She clasped my hand and smiled, but her gaze was intense. "No matter what happens, Trinity, don't ever forget that."

"I won't," I said.

"The cake man is back!" Dad's voice rang out. "Dig out those sugar berries and let's eat!"

I put the necklace back in the velvet box and dropped it into my kite bag. Then I held out a bowl. "Did you order my birthday cake from Zally's mom?"

"Yes, I did," Dad said. "They'll deliver it tomorrow night when Zally comes over."

"Cool." My mouth watered just thinking about it.

After dinner, Dad went into his study to prep for his trip to Orlando. Mom and I sat in the living room with popcorn and hot chocolate, watching a documentary about the Wright brothers. We had seen it before, but it was one of our favorites.

The Wright brothers were not, as many think, the first men to build a flying machine. They invented the controls that made fixed-wing flight possible, though, and they were the first to stay airborne under power for a long time.

"I guess people have always wanted to fly, huh?" I asked the question absently, not really looking for a reply.

"Yes, they have," Mom said.

"There is nothing more exhilarating than soaring through the sky."

"Is that how you feel in your jet?" I asked.

Mom laughed. "No, that's how I feel when I lock onto a strong air current that doubles my body speed in Aventurine. Like a surfer who finds the perfect wave in Hawaii."

"Oh, right." I watched the rest of the show without comment, trying to forget that my mom—an intelligent woman with a successful career—really thought she could fly.

At 9:55 I was logged onto my computer for my Skype date with Holly. She wasn't always on time, so I settled back to wait.

My gaze flicked past the velvet box on my nightstand to the kite bag hanging on the wall above my bed. Whenever my mother brought up Aventurine and her fantasy fairy life, my sense of reality shifted uncomfortably. The kite was real and gave me stability. It was the most important inanimate thing in my life, and one of only three things that decorated my walls.

I don't like clutter—in my thoughts or my surroundings.

A huge, framed photograph of my mother and me flying kites in New Zealand hung above my desk. Holly and several

21

other family friends were in it, too. Dad had taken the picture five years ago, capturing a moment of pure happiness. A traditional wood carving of a Maori fishhook hung beside the picture. To the Maori, the symbol represented strength, good luck, and safe travels over water. To me, it was a nice reminder of my ancestry.

"*Kia ora,* Trinity. I'm here!" Holly's beaming face appeared on my screen at 10:02.

"Hello back!" I grinned, thrilled to see her.

"I missed you so much today," Holly said.

"I miss you *every* day," I teased.

Holly faked a frown. "You know what I mean."

"Yep." I grinned. "Did you fly a kite at *Matariki*?"

"Of course I flew a kite!" Holly exclaimed. "That's the whole point of the festival. Did you?"

"Yes, in Central Park with Mom and Dad," I said. "Americans don't celebrate the New Year in May with kite flying, though. But the party they throw in Times Square is still pretty awesome. We might go next year to watch the ball drop. This year we just watched it on TV."

"That's cool. But I bet it won't be as much fun as *I* had today," Holly said with a mysterious smile.

Now I faked a frown. "How could you have fun? I wasn't there!"

Holly giggled. "But Anthony James was."

"Who's Anthony James?" I asked.

"My new boyfriend!" Holly squealed and bounced in her chair. "He is so cute I can't stand it!"

"But is he nice?" I asked.

"He's really nice," Holly said. "He's glad I'm smart, and he loves the fact that I like kites and horses and tramping through the woods more than I like clothes and makeup."

"Anthony sounds a lot better than the jerks I met in the park today," I said.

"Oh, that stinks. What made them jerks?"

"One of them called me a liar and the second one thought it was funny," I said. "But the third one wasn't so bad."

"Wait. You mean you met a boy you *like*?" Holly's eyes practically popped out of her head.

I just shrugged. "I'll probably never see Parker again, but I'm glad you found Anthony."

"Me too!" Holly sighed. "Anthony is taking me to the movies, so I have to go. Can we do this again tomorrow? I'm going to have so much to tell you!"

"Same time," I agreed. "Three of my new friends are sleeping over for my birthday. I can't wait for you to meet them."

After I signed off, I went into the bathroom to

brush my teeth. When I walked back into my room, Mom was sitting on the edge of my bed, holding the necklace.

"Is everything okay?" I asked. She hadn't tucked me into bed since I was seven.

"It's in a mother's nature to worry about her child," Mom said.

"You don't have to worry about me, Mom." I perched on the bed beside her. "I've got too much common sense to get into trouble."

"Perhaps, but"—Mom paused, then gripped my hand—"you are so certain of so much, Trinity, and that might be your greatest weakness."

"What?" I inhaled sharply. Nobody had ever accused me of being weak, and hearing it from my mother hurt.

"We have to recognize our weaknesses before we can deal with them," Mom explained. "Dealing with them makes us strong."

"I don't understand," I mumbled.

"Life isn't always neat and orderly," she went on. "One day, it will defy your expectations and force you to confront things that don't fit the world as you understand it. When that happens, you'll have to reassess what you think you know and adapt—or you will fail."

"I can adapt," I said stubbornly.

Mom watched me in silence for a moment. Then she asked, "Would you wear the necklace tonight?"

"Sure," I said. I didn't want to, but I knew it would make Mom happy. She smiled as she slipped the necklace around my neck, and I held up the back of my hair so she could fasten the clasp.

When she finished, I slipped under the sheets and closed my eyes. It had been a long, busy day, and I was exhausted.

My mother spoke again as I drifted off to sleep.

"Remember everything I've said about Aventurine, Trinity. I think I've told you everything you'll need to know. . . ."

3

Dream Walking

I flew high over a rolling landscape of forests, meadows, rivers, and lakes, arms spread to catch the air currents, my long brown hair streaming out behind me. A flock of geese called, welcoming me to their sky. The sun glinted off water below, daring me to dive. I pulled my arms in tight and arrowed downward, relishing the burst of speed and the sting of wind on my face as I plunged. . . .

I hit the ground and awakened with a start.

"What?" I sat up, heart pounding. I had been having vivid flying dreams for as long as I could remember, but I had never fallen before. The effect was startling, and a few seconds passed before I realized the crash landing wasn't the only difference.

I wasn't sitting on crisp clean sheets in my bedroom, but rather I was on ground covered with twigs, pebbles, and grass. My breath caught in my throat as

I glanced around. It was too dark to see much, but I could tell that I was wearing my clothes from earlier that day and the Ananya necklace.

Why? I felt panic rising in my chest. Inhaling deeply, I calmed myself so I could think clearly. There had to be a logical explanation.

For some reason, I had gotten dressed and sleep-walked my way back to Central Park. . . .

Or I was still dreaming.

I pinched myself.

It hurt.

But I didn't wake up in my bed.

I *was* outside, but where?

I sat still and used my other senses to gather more information. The scent of flowers mingled with the tang of woodsy decay. And I couldn't hear the rumble of traffic. Except for the crickets chirping and a soft gurgle of water, the land around me was quiet.

Too quiet, I thought with a shudder, *and totally creepy.*

Did I really leave our apartment and wander off in my sleep? The evidence seemed conclusive: I was deep inside Central Park.

I had never sleepwalked before. Why had I started now?

Unless I hadn't!

Another plausible theory popped into my head.

Mom was worried that I couldn't adapt to strange and unusual situations if the need arose. What if she had brought me out here to test me?

That has to be it, I decided. Nothing else made sense.

I knew she wouldn't leave me to face the dangers of the park alone. Mom was nearby, watching to see what I would do, ready to rescue me from harm.

Convinced I had figured it out, I was determined not to fail.

As the minutes passed, my eyes adjusted to the darkness and I could make out shadowy shapes. I was surrounded by trees with graceful branches that drooped to the ground, like the weeping willows by the boathouse pond.

These trees grew on the banks of a stream. I couldn't see it, but I could hear water tumbling over rocks.

A flickering light caught my eye as a cluster of fireflies emerged from the trees. They cast a remarkably bright glow, and I could see that the ground under the willows ahead was clear—almost like a path. I didn't hesitate. If I wanted to get home before dawn, I couldn't waste time.

Confident my mother would keep me in her sight, I rose to my feet and took several steps toward the fireflies. The movement disturbed them, and they escaped back into the trees. But I had moved far enough to see a dim gleam of light on the far side of the willow woods.

Light equaled safety and civilization. I walked toward it, using my hands to push willow branches out of my path.

As I got closer, the quiet was broken by a whispering hum. It sounded like the hummingbirds that hovered to drink from Zally's nectar feeder. I pressed on—until the hum became a buzz.

Bees?

I stopped. I wasn't allergic to bees, but I didn't want to be stung.

Then I heard a melodious, feminine laugh.

"Mom?" I spoke without thinking.

"Who-oo?" someone who wasn't my mother asked.

I didn't answer. If Mom was scoring me, I had just lost points for alerting someone to my presence.

I waited. Nothing moved, so I cautiously continued on toward what I could now make out as women's voices.

Had my mother brought friends to witness what must be an Ananya family initiation? Given everything she'd said before I'd fallen asleep, I should have guessed. She didn't want me to fail, so she had practically told me what to expect without actually telling me!

I spotted a lighted clearing beyond the gloomy shadows of the willows and hung back, studying the scene so I wouldn't do anything embarrassing.

Lanterns that seemed to hang suspended in mid-air were spaced around the perimeter of the glen. A large stone table stood at the center. Several beautiful women with wings entered the clearing from the woods.

"That's not my mother," I gasped, and closed my eyes, certain I had stumbled upon a bunch of weirdo women dressed up like fairies!

"Who-oo?" The voice spoke from above.

"What?" I asked in a choked, frightened whisper. "Who's there?"

"Who?" the voice asked.

I looked up into the golden-green eyes of a morepork owl, the only native owl left in New Zealand. Sitting on the limb of a nearby tree, the bird fluffed its golden-brown feathers and blinked. In Maori lore, the *ruru* was a guardian creature that screeched to warn of danger and death. The quieter *who-oo* call foretold good news. It was just a myth, but I was still relieved.

"Who are you?" the bird asked.

30

"Trinity Jones," I answered. "Who are you?"

"Tiaki," the bird said.

I blinked, stunned as much by the talking owl as by his name. In Maori, *tiaki* meant to care for or guard.

"Guard me against what?" I asked.

"Ignorance," Tiaki said. "I was sent to make sure you understand the great significance of this gathering of fairy queens."

I stared at the bird. A moment ago I thought I was walking through Central Park. This talking owl was making that harder and harder to believe.

"This is the strangest dream I've ever had," I muttered.

"A dream brought you to Aventurine," Tiaki said, "but you are not dreaming now."

I *had* to be dreaming, but I didn't argue. "Okay, then," I said. "What's the big deal?"

"Listen." The owl turned his head as the fairies gathered around the table.

The queens glided toward the table on shimmering wings. Some wore flowered wreaths and all wore gowns that complemented their wings. A tall fairy carrying a golden stick had leather twined into braids that were wrapped around her head. Another looked like a rock star, with long wavy red hair, cat eyeglasses, a leather jacket, and high leather boots.

One queen shimmered in silver from head to toe. Although their clothing, hairstyles, and accessories differed, they all had a regal presence, even a little girl at the edge of the group.

"One of the queens is a child!" I exclaimed.

"That's Queen Blanca," the owl said. "She takes a child's form sometimes. Most of the time she's a small white horse."

"Awesome!"

A tall fairy came toward the gathering from the other side of the clearing. She wore a lavender gown accented with sparkling dewdrops and violets. Cascades of chestnut hair fell in front of her shoulders and down her back between iridescent blue wings, and bees circled her head like a crown. The other queens parted to make room for her in the circle around the stone table.

She was obviously in charge.

"Is that Queen Patchouli?" I asked Tiaki in a whisper. The magnificent fairy looked exactly like my mother had described her.

"Yes," the owl said. "Queen of the Willowood Fairies and leader of all the queens in Aventurine."

"Why are there so many?" I asked.

"Every human fairy godmother lineage is bonded to a different fairy clan, and every clan has a queen," the bird explained. "Each queen trains fairy-godmothers-to-be in the magic arts that are particular to her clan and lineage."

"Which queen is in charge of the Ananya Lineage?" I asked.

"She is not here," Tiaki said. "Yet."

Why was my queen absent? Was she sick or in trouble? I started to ask, but Tiaki hushed me when Queen Patchouli began to speak.

"In this, the one hundredth year since I and my sister first entered Aventurine, the dawn of a new reign is upon us," she said.

Whenever a question occurred to me, I asked it. Now was no exception. "Where did she come from?"

"Queen Patchouli was born in your world but chose to stay in Aventurine," Tiaki said. "She is the only half-human fairy."

"How did she become the leader?"

"Every century marks a time of great change," the owl explained. "A hundred years ago, the portal between your world and Aventurine opened. Queen Patchouli's exceptional abilities and unique understanding of both human and fairy realms made her the most qualified to oversee young fairy-godmothers-in-training."

My mother hadn't told me anything about Queen Patchouli's history, and I listened closely when the fairy continued.

"Together," Queen Patchouli said, "Dora in the human world and I here among the fairies have helped you train three generations of fairy godmothers to respect and wield the magic of the elements."

"It has been an honor." The statuesque fairy wearing laced boots and a tunic raised her golden stick in salute.

Anticipating my next question, Tiaki whispered, "Queen Mangi of the stone fairies."

Queen Mangi spread her arms and bowed slightly. "Your faith in Kerka helped her achieve the Peace of Opposites and kept the Pax Lineage from being banned."

Kerka was the name of a girl at my new school, but I didn't know her very well. I decided I should make more of an effort.

"The credit for that is yours more than mine, Queen Mangi," Queen P said. "You were her guide and teacher."

"But you see the true hearts and spirits hidden beneath the girls' flaws." The silver fairy rose slightly on silvery wings laced with green, red, and blue. "Sumi seemed so hopeless at first."

"My friend Sumi?" I asked.

"Yes," Tiaki said. "She was quite superficial and fixated on outer beauty when she arrived."

"Not the Sumi I know!" I hissed in protest. "My Sumi sees beauty in all sorts of crazy places!"

"A gift she discovered when Queen Kumari turned her into a shape-shifter and sent her on an undersea quest to save Bristolmeir." The bird ruffled his feathers and turned back to the gathering.

"You sent Zally to save *me*, Queen Patchouli," a gentle voice said.

This time I didn't ask. Aventurine had been on my mind when I fell asleep, and I was incorporating my friend's fanciful stories about Shell Fairies into the dream, too.

Queen Patchouli gazed at a small fairy who had blind, white eyes. "Zally helped you regain your ability to heal, Queen Carmina. In return, you helped me empower her map of Aventurine, which benefits every girl who enters."

"Without the moonbeam basket Lilu wove, the Tangerine Tide would have destroyed the marsh," another queen added. Her kimono was alive with movement as animals swarmed, skittered, and swam through the fabric. "Surely you knew she could help the Dragonfly Fairies save it, Queen Patchouli."

"I *hoped* Lilu would find her own identity and the confidence to use her talents, and she did, with your encouragement, Queen Alaina." Queen Patchouli paused to scan the faces before her. "I know not what great change is in store, but rest assured: Our work with the human lineages will continue in the reign of my successor."

"I can't bear the thought of you leaving us!" the fairy who looked like a rock star shouted in dismay.

"I'm not leaving just yet, Queen Honorae," Queen Patchouli said. "The new baby will have years of training here in the Willowood Forest before she becomes Queen of Aventurine."

"Which one is having a baby?" I asked.

"Fairies do not have mothers and fathers like humans," the owl explained. "They are born of the elements and arrive as anything from mist or light to gem or flower."

I frowned. "The queens look like people."

"Babies materialize into fairy form when they are held by a fairy-godmother-in-training." Tiaki turned to study me.

The owl's stare was so intense I looked away.

In the clearing, an air of excitement had replaced the fairy queens' distress. All eyes looked up when Queen Patchouli raised her arms. A swirling mist of rainbow colors rose out of the stone table and transformed into a transparent three-dimensional diagram above it. The diagram was divided into many parts, and each part had a picture in it. I could just make out a shell, a dragonfly, and a willow.

"Does each section represent a fairy clan?" I asked.

"Most of them do," Tiaki said. "But others who are not fairies have territory in Aventurine, too."

All the queens except Queen Patchouli were acting like little kids waiting for Christmas. They whispered and grinned, crossed fingers and jiggled.

"What's going on?" I asked.

"They are about to find out where the new Queen of all Aventurine will be born," Tiaki explained. "It's a huge honor, and they all hope the baby will come to be in their land."

Everyone became quiet when Queen Patchouli began to chant:

Earth, water, fire, and air,
A new queen arising,
Show us where.

I held my breath as a brilliant blue cometlike light shot out of the table and up through the diagram to the uppermost section, where it burst into glorious fireworks.

All the fairies gasped.

"Oh, no!" Tiaki cried.

"This can't be!" Queen Mangi exclaimed.

"The elements don't lie," Queen Alaina said. As though sensing her great sadness, the creatures in her kimono became still.

My heart fluttered. "What's wrong?"

The owl blinked, then blinked again, as though he couldn't believe his eyes, either. "The child will arrive in the Cantigo Uplands."

"Does a bad fairy live there or something?" I asked.

"No fairies have ever *been* there," Tiaki said. "The cloud people control the Cantigo Uplands, and no one else is allowed into their territory, especially fairies."

"But then—" Suddenly, I was as upset about the unexpected complication as the fairies. "How are the queens going to get the baby?"

"Trinity!" Queen Patchouli called my name. "You can come out now."

The instant I heard Queen Patchouli call my name, I knew: Aventurine was real.

Stunned, I frantically tried to make sense of it.

I dreamed I could fly because I wanted to so much, but that was just wishful thinking.

My mother and my friends actually *believed* in fairies. They weren't little kids, and they were all smart, so it wasn't likely they shared a crazy delusion.

I pinched myself again—hard.

It hurt and my nails left a red mark on my skin.

I wasn't dreaming.

Somehow, I had been transported to a strange place with beautiful ladies who looked like fairies.

And they were expecting me.

"What does she want?" I glanced up, but Tiaki was gone.

I hadn't heard the beat of wings as he flew away. The bird had disappeared so quickly and silently it seemed as though he had simply vanished. *Poof!*

Did he? The idea seemed preposterous—unless Aventurine wasn't bound by the laws of physics that ruled the regular world.

That rocked me even harder.

I was a mathematician! I dealt in logic, absolutes, and facts. How could I function if nothing worked like I expected?

"One day, life will defy your expectations and force you to confront things that don't fit the world as you understand it. . . ." My mother's words were like a beacon shining through a thick fog. Knowing what was ahead, she had armed me to cope and succeed. *"Reassess what you think you know and adapt."*

"New fact number one," I muttered. "In Aventurine, anything might be possible."

I took a deep breath and stepped out of the trees.

All the queens turned to look my way. I tensed, but there was no need to be wary. I could see their faces in the lighted clearing, and every one had a hopeful, if anxious, look.

Queen Patchouli held out a welcoming hand. "Stand with me, Trinity. There is much to tell and not much time to tell it."

Before she could continue, I double-checked my theory. "Is this Aventurine?"

"Yes, it is," Queen Patchouli answered. "Your mother and grandmother were here when they turned thirteen, and they both earned high marks and much respect for the Ananya Lineage. However, they did not have missions that were as vital to the future of Aventurine as you."

I paused, recalling my mother's account of her amazing mission. She had carried the fallen egg of a dinosaur-like creature back to its nest. The nest had been located on a mountain crag that was so high and remote she had to fly to complete the task.

"What is the mission?" I asked.

"As I'm sure Tiaki told you, a baby who is destined to be Queen of Aventurine is about to be born," Queen Patchouli explained. "In order to materialize, she must be held by a fairy-godmother-in-training—you."

"Really?" My voice squeaked with excitement. I didn't know anything about babies, but holding one couldn't be that hard.

Except that the newborn was arriving in the Cantigo Uplands.

"What about the cloud people?" I asked. "Tiaki said they don't like strangers."

"They don't like anyone," Queen Kumari grumbled.

"They're mean," the child Queen Blanca said, knitting her brow.

"They are fierce warriors," Queen Mangi added. "The combat arts of Kalis might help, but there's no time to teach you." She spun her glowing stick and then held it like a spear.

"Why are they so hostile?" I asked. Knowing why might help me survive.

"They are beings made of mist, and like the Greek gods of your world, they consider themselves and their ways superior," the golden queen explained.

"It's worse than that, Queen Tensy," Queen Honorae said. "They don't want *anything* to change."

"They especially don't want to be solid," the queen in the beaded dress huffed.

"You are so right about that, Mama Cocha," Queen Alaina said. "The cloud people are convinced that intruders bring change, chaos, and ruin. Sadly, human history has often proven their theory."

"But we would not do them any harm," Queen Carmina said. "We only want to peacefully coexist as we do with all the others who are not fairies in Aventurine."

"Most of them anyway," Mama Cocha muttered.

"Maybe the new queen will open a door," Queen Blanca said with a wistful sigh.

"Not likely," Queen Mangi scoffed. "Trinity and the babe will be lucky to escape with their lives."

"Is it that dangerous?" I didn't like the sound of that.

"Everything you need to bring the baby back to the Willowood for her naming ceremony will be available," Queen Patchouli said. With a flick of her wrist, the spelled map shattered into sparkling confetti that dissolved before it hit the stone table. "But first you must make the journey up through the mile-high forest to reach the land of clouds."

"I love to climb trees!" I exclaimed. "I don't mean to brag, but I'm very good at it."

"That's one reason why you were chosen," Queen Patchouli said. "But the trees will only take you so far. You'll have to fly to complete the journey."

"Fly?" I asked. "Using what?"

The queen's smile was not reassuring. "You'll know when you get there."

A flicker of doubt must have crossed my face. Queen Patchouli's voice took on an even greater sense of urgency.

"No mission has ever been more important," she explained. "This baby will be born with immense power, but it must be tempered with the guidance and training only the Willowood Fairies and I can provide. Without it, she won't have the wisdom to manage all the creatures and magical forces in Aventurine."

"The harmony in Aventurine will disintegrate without a wise, strong, and powerful leader," Queen Mangi said. "Mist or solid, the baby must not be stranded with the cloud people."

"I will not let that happen." I tried to speak with the certainty of a knight charged with a sacred duty. I could not let my mother, our lineage, or the fairy realm down.

4

From Here to There

The queens all smiled—some even cheered—but I kept my eyes on Queen Patchouli. She seemed to be weighing me with her gaze, and I wondered if I was coming up lacking.

Thousands of fireflies gathered to brighten the clearing. Morning flowers bloomed in the light, and the stones in the table began to shift until a crude desk and stool appeared before me.

"Now you must make your entry into *The Book of Dreams*," Queen Patchouli said. "Please, sit."

"Dreams that I've dreamed or dreams about what I want?" I

asked as I sat down on the cool, smooth rock.

"Aren't they the same?" Queen Patchouli asked with a mischievous twinkle in her eye.

"I can dream the impossible," I replied, "but I can't make the impossible happen no matter how much I want it."

"Perhaps," the queen said, "just this once, you should think as though nothing is impossible."

Adapt! I reminded myself. "Okay," I said. "I guess I can do that."

Two new fairies entered the clearing. One set a large, leather-bound book on the desk before me. The silver-blue letters on the cover shimmered, and stray pieces of ribbon and dried flowers stuck out of the aged pages. The second fairy placed a golden quill pen and shell beside it. The lid on the shell was decorated with fish scales. It opened without me touching it. The book did, too.

Queen Patchouli peered over my shoulder. "This is your mother's dream. I am certain she thought it quite impossible when she wrote it."

Mom's page was covered with small drawings of flying machines: kites, balloons, hang gliders, biplanes, propeller planes, jets, and helicopters. The images were decorated with what looked like the flax and grasses the Maori used to make kites. I skimmed over the designs to read:

My dream is to open my father's heart and eyes. Let him see that I am as smart as my brothers and deserve to go to college. I can learn to fly if given the chance.

—Marissa

"She did, you know." I looked at Queen Patchouli. "Mom is a commercial airline pilot, and those jobs are usually held by men."

"I know," Queen Patchouli said. "We're very proud of Marissa. Now it's your turn."

The book opened to a blank page. I picked up the golden pen and dipped it into the silvery-blue ink, but I hesitated before writing.

I wanted to fly, but not in airplanes like my mother. I wanted to fly under my own power with no external help. But, despite Queen Patchouli's advice, I didn't feel comfortable writing that. It seemed too frivolous for a book that had recorded generations of girls' innermost secret desires.

What did I really want out of life?

Ever since I was little, my mother had told me that I could be and do anything I wanted. All the women in our family had achieved their sky-high dreams and aspirations.

I dipped the pen in the ink again and wrote:

I want to reach new heights in the field of mathematics by contributing something that expands knowledge and makes the world a better place, like Einstein and his theory of relativity and Sally Ride, the first American woman astronaut, whose work with gravity helped prove that Einstein was correct.

—Trinity

I put the pen down and smiled with satisfaction. I didn't expect my dream to come true because I wrote it in a book. Like my mother, I'd have to work hard to make it happen. Still, I liked the idea that my daughter might read my words someday, especially if I succeeded.

Thoughts about my illustrious future receded as pictures began to appear on the borders of my page. Unlike the flying devices surrounding Mom's dream, my words were decorated with images of flying creatures: birds, butterflies, and dragons. Ribbons like those that I had woven into my kite wound in and around the pictures. I loved the design, but it made me uneasy, too.

Does the book know that my real number-one dream is to fly?

The heavy leather cover lifted and closed with a thud. Dust and bits of dried leaves whooshed from between the pages. Before the cloud settled, the two fairies took the book, the quill, and the ink shell away.

"What's next?" I asked Queen Patchouli. Now that I had moved past my this-can't-possibly-be-happening frame of mind, I was eager to get going.

"Now we must get you properly outfitted." Queen Patchouli waved me to follow as she headed out of the clearing. The other queens fell into line behind us as we entered a dense thicket of willows.

In the dark, I could see a golden aura that surrounded the Queen of Aventurine. The glow had been hidden by torchlight in the clearing, but here it kept me from stumbling off the path. Her aura faded when we entered the outskirts of a village.

The path we had followed through the woods gradually melded into a road embedded with gems, polished stones, seashells, and crystals. Quaint dwellings made of thatch, flowers, vines, stones, shells, and woven willow branches had been built at varying distances from the road. Most were firmly on the ground, but a few floated while others hung from trees like swings. Shadows shimmered in flickering firefly light. Torches blazed along the road, and lantern bugs cast light wherever they flew.

Queen Patchouli stopped when she reached a crooked house at the center of the village. Made of willow branches, feathers, ribbons, and grass, it resembled an upside-down bird's nest.

"You'll find the wardrobe inside," Queen Patchouli said. "Choose whatever you want to wear."

I hoped the wardrobe had what I needed: hiking boots with textured soles so I wouldn't slip, a long-sleeved shirt, and snug pants to protect my arms and legs.

"I'll wait out here," Queen P said, urging me to get moving without actually saying so.

Taking the hint, I hurried down the stone path. The door into the nest house was made of long feathers and grass streamers. After I parted the strands and stepped inside, the streamers fused into a solid panel.

So I wouldn't try to escape? Or because it wouldn't let me out until I picked a suitable outfit for climbing?

A tree stump in the center of the room cracked open, drawing my attention. Emerging from the crack was a wooden panel that rose until it stopped a foot short of the ceiling. Then, as I watched with my mouth hanging open in disbelief, the panel unfolded and expanded until it became a huge cabinet with two doors on top and three drawers below. Carvings of tall pine trees stretched up the doors, and a beautiful kite decorated the top.

I didn't move, not even when the wardrobe suddenly popped open. I stared at the fantastic collection of skirts, blouses, shirts, leggings, boots, shoes, scarves, and hats that hung on pegs and overflowed the drawers. Gossamer fabrics were mingled with sturdy homespun threads. Some of the clothes were accented with jewels, feathers, or beads. There were so many choices, it was impossible to choose. As though realizing I needed a nudge, a long-sleeved white tunic dropped off a hanger and fell on the floor at my feet. It was beautifully woven and as soft as a cloud. The white would be a good camouflage when I reached the Cantigo Uplands.

The tunic needed leggings, so I found a pair with a fun pattern that reminded me of Maori tattoos. They were tan and wouldn't stick out on the tree or in the clouds.

When I finished, a mirror appeared on the front of the wardrobe. Placing my hands on my hips, I regarded myself from all angles and nodded with approval.

The white and tan clothes that I had chosen would provide excellent camouflage in the clouds. The greenstone beads and ivory disk of the Ananya necklace lacked the brilliance of most jewelry, but it shone against the bright white tunic. However, if I had to blend in, I could hide the compass disk inside my new shirt.

"I guess that's it," I said to myself.

The wardrobe seemed to agree. In the space of a few seconds, it condensed and folded itself back into the tree stump. When I turned to leave, the nest house door had become loose feather and grass streamers again.

Satisfied I had chosen well, I left the house with renewed confidence.

Queen Patchouli was waiting for me outside. She was alone, but as I approached, the other two fairies returned with a large basket. They set it on a toadstool.

Queen Patchouli didn't comment on my clothing choices. I took her silence as approval and gave her my full attention when she mentioned gifts.

"Every fairy-godmother-in-training is given three things she'll need to complete her mission," Queen Patchouli explained as she pulled a spool of string out of the basket.

I don't know what I was expecting, but it wasn't string. If Queen Patchouli noticed my disappointment, she didn't let on.

"This string will never break," the queen said, "but you can cut it. You must make a kite as soon as you reach the lower branches of the trees. You'll need one to reach the Cantigo Uplands, and this string might come in handy."

"What if I can't find the materials I need for the kite?" I didn't want to start off on a negative note, but the question had to be asked.

"Improvise," Queen Patchouli said. She reached into the basket again, discouraging further discussion.

I didn't have any pockets, which was a huge mistake on my part. I couldn't climb if I had to carry stuff, but Queen Patchouli had that problem covered. My second gift was a beautifully beaded belt with a harness backpack attached to the back.

"The harness is designed to hold the kite," Queen Patchouli went on. "The backpack contains an always-full water pod and a never-gone sweet potato so you won't go thirsty or hungry."

"Thanks," I said. I didn't tell her that sweet potatoes were on my yuck list. I didn't even eat the traditional marshmallow-covered ones Mom made for my first American Thanksgiving last November. Still, I'd eat the fairy's sweet potato if I got hungry enough.

My third present was a feather that Queen Patchouli wove into my hair by my left ear.

"What does the feather do?" I asked.

"It will be quite useful under certain circumstances."

The queen's answer didn't tell me anything. I started to ask what circumstances, but she gracefully waved her arms, cutting me off. The bees abandoned their lazy circles about her head and flew away. A few minutes later, they came back with the other fairy queens.

As the first rays of daylight peeked through the

trees, the queens formed a circle around me. They held hands and began to chant:

> *Mirror, mirror, let her go*
> *Through your glass to reach the bough.*
> *Mirror, mirror, let her go*
> *Safely to fulfill her vow.*

A large oval mirror appeared and hovered six inches off the ground. I wasn't sure exactly what the spell meant, but I could see myself and the fairies reflected in the glass.

"The fastest way to reach the mile-high forest is through the Portal of Magic Mirrors," Queen Patchouli said. "Once you enter, you'll be taken to the tree you must climb to reach the Cantigo Uplands."

"Cool!" I couldn't help being excited. The quest was clearly going to be tough, but I was determined to rise to the challenge.

"You must *not* open your eyes until you are through the mirror." Queen Patchouli's warning was delivered in a harsh, no-nonsense tone. "Just go with the flow."

I nodded and took a deep breath. "Do I go through now?"

"Whenever you're ready," Queen Patchouli said. "Good luck, Trinity."

I took another deep breath, squeezed my eyes shut, and stepped through the mirror. I kept expecting to bump my nose on the glass. Then, since that didn't happen, I automatically considered possible scientific explanations for the phenomenon. I suspected the magic portal was actually a wormhole, a passage through the space-time continuum that would deliver me to the distant forest.

Overwhelmed by curiosity, I wanted to look. But I decided it wouldn't be wise to ignore Queen Patchouli's instructions the moment my mission began. *That* turned out to be a good call. In less than a second, I was yanked off my feet, wrapped in a cocoon of warm air, and hurled like I had been shot from a cannon.

The ride was worse than the Cyclone roller coaster on Coney Island. I couldn't see, but I felt every jolt, sudden turn, updraft, downdraft, stop, and acceleration. The sensations were so terrifying it took every ounce of willpower I had to keep my eyes closed. My imagination, however, ran wild as I hurtled through the mirror-world gauntlet.

I saw myself passing mirror after mirror with no more than a hairbreadth margin. The slightest deviation would send me off course and crashing into glass. I tensed and tried not to flinch as I was jerked to the right and then to the left to avoid unknown obstacles.

Even when it felt like I was slowing down, I kept

my eyes closed. Somehow, I knew that the air tube would rocket off again. Dizzy and nauseous, I just wanted the ride to be over.

How will I know it's over? I wondered. *When I stop, should I wait ten seconds or ten minutes?*

Suddenly, the air cocoon jerked to a complete stop, then unraveled and dumped me.

That's how, I thought when I hit the ground. I waited for a minute before I dared look, and then I squinted without fully opening my eyes. It probably wouldn't save me if I was opening my eyes too soon, but the smell of musky pine made me feel like I was safely through the portal. Through slitted eyes, I could see that I was right. I was facing a roughly textured wall of mottled brown and gray.

Bark, I realized when I touched it. The portal had delivered me to the climbing tree in the mile-high forest as Queen Patchouli promised.

Exhaling, I relaxed and studied my new surroundings. A strip of sand twelve feet wide separated the dense woods from the humongous pine tree before me. The trunk stretched as far as I could see on both sides. I craned my neck to look up. The lowest branch was so high it seemed no bigger than a toothpick. Turning, I expected to see a mirror-exit behind me, but there were only more pine trees. They were normal size but packed so closely together they formed an impenetrable barrier. The only way to go was up, but I had no idea how to reach the first branch. I leaned against the rough bark to puzzle out the problem.

Back home in New Zealand, I went to the indoor climbing wall every week, and my dad and I had spent several mountain-climbing weekends in Fiordland National Park. Scaling a vertical surface wasn't impossible with regular climbing gear.

The lead climber inserted protection devices into a crack in the rock and secured ropes to them with carabiners. Everyone wore a harness that was connected to the rope. The equipment and techniques were designed to prevent falls.

I ran my fingers over the monster tree's bark. The grooves were as deep as cracks in a rock face, but I didn't have the equipment.

A movement on the side of the tree caught my eye. A purple caterpillar clung to the bark with dozens of sticky feet. Six inches long with twitching yellow eyestalks, it wasn't moving fast, but it was moving.

I'm in Aventurine, I reminded myself, *and the rules are different.* I had to think like a fairy, and it seemed that fairies took their cues from nature. Maybe my fingers would magically turn into suckers if I just started climbing.

With nothing to lose, I adjusted the harness on

my back and took a few deep breaths. Then I placed the bottom of my shoe on the bark. When I lifted my other foot, I didn't magically grip the side of the tree. I fell back down.

"Scratch sticky feet," I muttered.

Stumped, I looked in both directions. The surface of the massive tree trunk looked unbroken all the way to the horizon, but distance could warp things. Sometimes what appears flat actually isn't.

I couldn't go up so I had to go right or left.

But which way?

I counted to ten and reverted back to Trinity thinking—logically. The Queen of Aventurine would not have sent me on a mission that couldn't be accomplished.

I drew a total blank.

I had to be missing something, and it was probably something obvious. I sat down and looked right. I watched and listened for several minutes. There was nothing to notice except the monotony of the brown-gray bark.

I looked left. A minute passed before I saw the dots in the distant sky. The dots could be birds.

A few seconds later, I heard a faint *rat-a-tat-tat*. *Hammer?* I wondered. *Or woodpecker?* Either way, something was happening on or near the tree on the left. I didn't pause to think about my decision. I couldn't afford to doubt my instincts. I headed toward the dots.

I walked with no way to judge distance or time. I didn't know if two, three, or four hours had passed when I saw wings on the dots. The closer I got to the flying things, the more creatures appeared on the tree trunk.

In addition to purple caterpillars, I saw tiny flowers with prickly leaves, red corkscrew bugs, and trickles of sap. The *rat-a-tat-tat* sound came from furry little animals with long sharp claws. The red bugs drilled, and the furry things drummed the bark with their claws to make the sap flow. Apparently, sap was a food source.

Brown and gray with bright orange beaks, the birds circled like vultures waiting for dinner to die. I wondered if it had been a good idea to go this way, but as I neared the birds, I could see a strange pattern in the bark ahead.

"Finally!" I exclaimed when I saw the winding staircase that had been carved into the trunk.

Unfortunately, a tangle of vines several feet wide grew over the lower steps. I could easily scramble over it, but my mother's stories had made clear that Aventurine was riddled with nasty surprises. I decided to wait a bit before touching the vines; something about the vultures made me wary.

A black beetle with snapping jaws poked its head out of the vines, and the vultures dived. One of the birds was fast, aiming right for the beetle. At the last moment, the beetle ducked back into the vines, and the vulture's beak snapped shut on empty air. It screamed in frustration and pumped its wings to circle back up to its friends.

I shivered, wondering how many biting bugs were waiting for a tender girl to crawl over the vines. Still, I knew I had to do it. The stairs were the only way to climb the tree.

"But I don't have to serve myself up as bug breakfast." I spoke aloud to settle my rattled nerves. Thinking about breakfast made me hungry. I hadn't eaten since dinner at home in New York. That had probably only been hours ago, but it felt like days.

I sat down and took out the water pod and sweet potato. When I poked the top of the pod, it split open at the top. I held it to my lips and drank. The water was cold and had a hint of lemon. It immediately quenched my thirst. I turned to the sweet potato. It looked normal, but obviously it was also magical.

I poked it like I had poked the water pod and a dent formed. I dug a finger into the dent and a large chip flaked off. I bit off a corner and smiled. It was delicious. The sweet potato chip was both sweet and savory, like a sugary potato chip, but somehow I could tell it was nourishing. One chip was enough; I was completely full.

I began to study the vines. Every time a beetle popped out, a vulture tried to catch it. The birds almost never succeeded, and the threat didn't stop the beetles from popping up like Whac-A-Moles.

When I opened the backpack to put away my food and water, I saw the spool of string and had an inspiration. If I could clear even the smallest path through the vines, this would give the birds the advantage, as they could reach the beetles for a couple minutes; the beetles might stay hidden long enough for me to quickly climb over the vines.

I didn't have a knife or cutting tool, but Queen Patchouli said I could cut the string, so I could probably use anything. Standing up, I measured a piece four times my height and then found a groove in the bark. The edge easily cut the string.

I threaded the string carefully around a heavy vine

and tied it tight. Then I walked over to the edge
of the sand strip, where the smaller pine trees
blocked the way, and looped the string over
a low-hanging branch. Then I gripped the
string tight and began walking back toward
the vine.

With each step, the string was pulled
more taut. And slowly the vine began to move
toward the branch and away from the
steps. After years of growing into the stairs,
it resisted, but Queen Patchouli
had insisted that the string
wouldn't break unless I cut it,
so I was confident that if I just kept
walking, the vine would clear away.

Step by careful step, I shifted the vine
and cleared a sliver of a path. Beetles scattered
as their cover lifted, and a few vultures were
finally successful at gobbling them up. I quickly
tied my end of the string to the newly moved
vine, creating a taut loop.

I rushed up the path, trying not to
trip over the small tendrils of vines
beginning to creep back over the
stairs I had cleared. Heart thumping, I
kept climbing until I was far above the vines.

When I turned, the tendrils had thickened and the

path was completely closed off. Only the unbreakable loop of string from the vine to the branch showed my passing. I had been lucky that I was quick enough not to be trapped beneath the vines. I caught my breath and then decided there was no going back. I could only head up, so I started to climb.

I took my time, checking my footing and making sure I didn't touch anything in the bark that might nip, slime, or sting. The lowest branch seemed very far away, but it wasn't as high as the toothpick branch where I had landed. The fact that someone had carved stairs gave me hope that I would make it to the top.

When I stopped to rest, I couldn't tell how high I had climbed. The forest landscape was cloaked in gray mist. I had a fantastic view of the sky above it, however, and it was growing darker.

Despite the dangers, I quickened my pace. I did not want to be stuck on the stairs with no protection at night. Once I reached the tree branch, I could secure myself with the string and sleep without fear of falling.

As I got closer to the branch, my legs began to ache, but I didn't falter. After several grueling minutes, when I was only an arm's length away from my goal, a whizzing sound brought me to a halt. I hugged the tree, wondering what little horror Aventurine had in store for me next.

A whirligig toy landed on the step at my feet.

I picked it up and smiled, impressed by the craftsmanship and design. It was made of woven leaves.

Then I realized what the whirligig really meant: I was not alone in the tree.

5

Friend or Foe

"You should have listened to me, Jango!" someone above me said. "It's just a little bad design flaw."

"You're not always right, Targa! Go away!" a slightly deeper voice answered.

"Fine! I have better things to do anyway," Targa said.

The talkers sounded like cute cartoon creatures. Still holding the toy, I climbed the last few steps up to the branch.

And came face to face with a puppy.

At least, that's what I thought at first glance. The creature had pointed ears with tufts of fur on the edges, a squashed muzzle with a black nose, and huge black eyes.

I assumed I was staring at Jango, who seemed

even more surprised to see me. He was so startled, he froze.

"G'day, Jango!" I greeted him with a smile. "Is this what you're looking for?"

Jango scowled and sniffed.

I had never owned a dog, but I knew their power of smell was thousands of times better than a human's. If the same was true of these beings, Jango could tell if I was friendly or not by my scent. He could also tell if I was afraid.

Show no fear was rule number one when confronted by a strange dog.

I held out the whirligig. "This is very well made. The tips just need to be turned up a little more."

Jango's scowl deepened. "That's what Targa said." He took the toy from my hand. Then he turned and scampered off on all fours down the branch.

Now I could see that he had the arms, legs, and body of a monkey—only more compact. A short bib-coverall made of a silky material and woven leaves covered his silver-black fur. His gripping paws were bare, and his curled tail looked like it could hold on to branches just like a monkey's.

The limb I had reached was so wide I couldn't see the other side. Hundreds of big secondary branches supported vines and other flowering foliage. A wide path had been worn in the thick bark, and many smaller paths branched out from it. Farther along the limb, wooden walkways and small rustic buildings were nestled in the branches.

I gawked for several seconds before I realized Jango was sounding the alert as he ran toward the village.

"Stranger on the tree!" Jango called out, and howled, warning the pack. "It looks like a bog fairy with no wings!"

"Stop telling stories, Jango!" a larger creature yelled down from a doorway. "There's not a Curipoo in the village who believes you about anything anymore."

I blinked when I heard what the beings were called. *Kuri* is the Maori word for "dog."

"Berto could use some biggle berries for tarts," another creature told Jango. "Get a bucket and pick some for him."

Jango stopped in the middle of the path. "But I'm not kidding!"

Both larger Curipoos shook their heads and went back inside their huts.

Jango spun, heaved a sigh, and started marching toward me.

I couldn't go back down, and I was too exhausted

to continue climbing. I sat and waited, hoping Jango didn't bite.

Jango stopped in front of me. Still on all fours, he thrust his head and shoulders forward, a stance that was intended to intimidate me. "You're still here."

"Yes, I am," I said.

"What are you?" Jango asked.

"My name is Trinity, and I'm a fairy-godmother-in-training," I said. "I'm on a mission for Queen Patchouli."

For the second time, Jango was paralyzed with surprise. He stared at me for several seconds before he found his voice again. "Come with me. The elders won't believe I found a fairy godmother unless they see it for themselves."

Jango spoke as though I didn't have a choice. I decided to go with him, but I had to set the record straight.

"I'm not a fairy godmother yet," I said as I followed him down the path.

"You've met Queen Patchouli!" Jango exclaimed. "So you are very, *very* important."

The young Curipoo paused until I walked alongside him.

"This is a big favor you are doing for me," Jango said. "I will not forget it."

"No favor," I said. "You found me fair and square."

Jango puffed out his chest. "Yes, I did."

As we neared the outskirts of the village, other Curipoo peeked out of huts or stood on walkways, gawking and sniffing.

I didn't sniff, but I gawked a lot.

The structures were not as primitive as they looked from afar, and they were not built with boards or logs. The huts had been carved out of huge gnarls in the limb, and the walkways were made of thin peels of wood and leaves, woven together and reinforced with vines. Balcony porches were decorated with intricate carvings of birds, insects, flowers, and flying contraptions like Jango's whirligig.

The tables, stools, and benches on the porches and in the rest of the alcoves along the walkways were carved or made of the same sturdy woven materials. Baskets overflowing with flowers hung at random on the lower paths. I didn't see a decorative carving that looked like a kite, but it was obvious why Queen Patchouli told me to make mine here. The Curipoo had everything I needed.

Before long, there was a curious crowd following us.

"Who is this stranger, Jango?"

I recognized Targa's voice. The young Curipoo with golden fur wore a short, silky shift dress decorated with carved nuts and wooden beads.

"This is Trinity. She's a fairy-godmother-in-training and my friend." As though to punctuate that point, Jango thrust his muzzle into my hand.

I scratched him under the chin.

"See?" Jango bragged.

Targa huffed, but she didn't back off. She was jealous, and she wasn't leaving Jango alone with an intriguing visitor.

"I'm very pleased to meet you, Targa," I said.

Targa's eyes widened. "You know my name!"

I leaned over to whisper, "You were right about altering the whirligig. Shhhh." I glanced at Jango. He was preoccupied explaining my presence to a larger Curipoo and didn't hear our exchange.

Judging by Jango's deference, the large brown and black male was someone important. He wore a long, open vest made of purple flowers and red leaves over a silky shirt and trousers. A jeweled amulet hung around his neck.

"Not a word," Targa whispered back with an impish grin. Then she brushed up against me; it felt like she was marking me as her friend, too. She was still smiling when Jango turned to introduce me.

"Mayor Mordo, may I present Trinity, a fairy-godmother-in-training and emissary of the great Queen Patchouli!" Jango's voice swelled with pride, and I thought his heart would burst when I replied.

"Jango does me a great honor with this introduction, Mayor Mordo." I bowed slightly and lowered my eyes to show I accepted his dominance in the village. It felt like the right thing to do.

"The honor is ours, Trinity." Mordo's voice was lower and husky. "We invite you to be our guest for food and lodging this night, and we very much hope you will tell us of your travels."

"And your meeting with the Queen of all Aventurine," Jango added.

The mayor growled and nudged the smaller Curipoo.

"I would love to tell you!" I exclaimed. "And thank you so much for your kind hospitality. I am hungry and tired. It's been a long day."

Snarls and yaps erupted when young Curipoo bumped heads looking at my shoes. In fact, half a dozen Curipoo toddlers were crawling around my feet or sitting and staring up at me in black-eyed baby awe.

The mayor scowled and barked, "Will you folks please watch your cubs?"

"They're adorable!" I patted each puppy head,

which sent them all scampering back to their parents. They were either scared out of their wits or anxious to show off.

Now that I had a size comparison, I was pretty sure Jango and Targa were closer to my age than the young kids I'd originally taken them for.

"There are sleeping slings in the Grand Hall if you'd like to rest before we eat," Mayor Mordo said.

"Actually, I'd like to help Jango and Targa pick biggle berries," I said. "They sound delicious."

"I make the best tarts on the tree!" An elderly Curipoo waved from the middle of the crowd.

"My friend is the best guest ever, right?" Jango asked.

"The best in a long time," the mayor agreed.

Targa rushed off and came back with three wooden buckets. "I know the best bushes."

Flanked by my two new companions, we ducked down a side path. We passed several shops that stocked all the supplies the Curipoo used to make everything they needed, most of which was available on the tree. The exceptions were bright-colored gems, metals, and rocks.

"That's the Precious Things store," Targa said. Then she whispered, "Someday Jango is going to get me a mate-for-life present there. He just doesn't know it yet."

"That's how it works with my people, too," I said with a grin. "Where do the precious things come from?"

"Very brave fathers, sons, and daughters go down the tree to find them," Jango explained. "There are many terrible dangers on the ground. That's why the things are so precious."

"I like beads better than shiny rocks any-way," Targa said. "I carve my own."

"Did you make the beads you're wear-ing?" I asked. "They're gorgeous!"

Targa pulled a wooden bead shaped like a rose off her dress and put it in my hand. "So you never forget me."

"I'll never forget you and Jango." I put the present in my pack so I wouldn't lose it. The bead was the best gift I had ever received.

"We're here!" Jango announced.

The biggle berry patch was on the outer edge of the limb, where there was more sun. The purple ber-ries were three times the size of regular blackberries and grew on thorny bushes.

Jango and Targa pushed through the tangled branches to get at the big clusters of berries on the sunny side of the patch. I quickly found out that a Curipoo's skin was protected by thick fur, but the needlelike thorns poked right through my clothes. I decided not to wade in any farther and picked the closer branches clean.

When our buckets were full, we hurried back to Berto's pastry shop in the village.

"Thank you so much, much!" Berto was ecstatic. "Now I have enough berries to bake tarts for everyone!"

"Will everyone buy one?" I asked.

"Buy?" Jango asked, puzzled. "What is that?"

"It's like a trade," I said. "People make things and other people buy the things with metal coins and paper money. Sometimes people make a deal and trade stuff. That's called bartering."

"Oh." Targa looked confused. "Everyone here does what they love to do. I make beads."

"Others carve houses or plant flowers or make clothes," Jango added.

"And we give what we do to anyone who needs it," Targa finished.

"I want to make flying toys," Jango said. "All the cubs love them."

"If they fly," Targa said.

Jango's brow furrowed, but I could tell he knew she had a point.

"Let's work on it tomorrow," she said.

"Okay."

Targa looked pleased, not victorious.

"I have to make a kite," I said. "Will you help me?"

"What's a kite?" they both asked.

"You'll see!" I teased.

Jango and Targa took me to a cozy room attached to the Grand Hall so I could clean up and rest. I washed the berry juice off my face and hands in rainwater that had been collected in a huge wooden tank. When I tugged a braided vine, water dribbled into a big shell set inside a carved pedestal. The Curipoo used the silky bark as washcloths, too. I brushed my teeth with a sweet-tasting twig. Then I stretched out in a hammock, covered myself with a blanket, and fell asleep.

Targa shook me awake. "The feast is ready, and everyone is waiting for the guest of honor."

I splashed water on my face and combed my hair with a wooden comb. Assuming I'd be sleeping in the same room that night, I left my harness and backpack in the hammock. Then I walked out into the biggest party I had ever seen.

It looked like every Curipoo who wasn't a child and home in bed had turned out to celebrate my visit.

The Grand Hall was a cavernous room in a huge, hollowed-out gnarl. Lanterns hung from decorative hooks and swirls carved into the ceiling. Mismatched tables, chairs, stools, and benches were haphazardly placed throughout the hall. Six musicians stood on a raised platform in one corner, playing lively music on gourd drums, wooden flutes, and stringed instruments. My stomach growled when I inhaled the delicious aromas drifting through the room.

The Curipoo must love to barbeque; they had cooked up a huge barbie.

A stone fire pit stretched along one-third of the far wall. Large vegetables roasted on a spit and pots of soup steamed over the coals. Berto and other bakers tended fresh breads and cakes that baked in small stone ovens. Chefs sat on the ends of the pit, adding spices and stirring the specialties they cooked in large wooden bowls that looked like Chinese woks. The woks were heated by flat stones that rested on the embers. When an entrée was finished, the chef poured it into a serving bowl on a long buffet table and started making something else. Diners helped themselves to whatever was available and then found a place to sit, chat, and eat in the hall or the gardens outside.

"It's a bring-a-plate!" I exclaimed. In New Zealand, everyone always brought food to share at a

party or picnic. I'd learned that Americans had similar parties called potluck dinners.

"Yes," Targa said. "Everyone brings their own
plate, cup, and utensils."

As Targa spoke, I realized that all the Curipoo
walking into the hall carried dishes.

"I don't have a plate," I whispered to Targa.

"It's been taken care of," Targa answered. "I hope
you're hungry."

"Famished!" I exclaimed.

I had no doubt that everything would taste just as
good as it smelled. When people do things they love,
they usually do it well.

"Trinity! Targa!" Jango waved from Mayor
Mordo's long table at the head of the room. He
picked up plates from the table and ran over to join
us. "Jobri just finished making crunchy bugs! If we
don't hurry, they'll be all gone."

I *hoped* they'd be gone, but they weren't. Jango
put a heaping spoonful on my plate. Then, with Jobri
watching, he urged me to try one. I couldn't refuse.
Bracing myself, I popped a crunchy
bug into my mouth, tried not
to grimace, and chewed. It
tasted like crispy, honey-
battered chicken.

"Oh, wow!" I exclaimed. "That's fantastic. *Fantastic!*"

"They're my favorite!" Jango beamed.

I couldn't pick a favorite. I ate two helpings of fruit salad with nectar dressing, three bread rolls with honey and jam, a roasted squash-type veggie, more crunchy bugs, and two of Berto's biggle berry tarts. After dinner, we had a warm cider drink sweetened with honeycomb wafers.

When Mayor Mordo finished eating, the serious conversation began. "What's Queen Patchouli like?" he asked.

"She's magnificent," I answered. "She has gorgeous long hair and glittering blue wings, and a swarm of bees that circle her head like a crown."

"But what is she like?" the mayor repeated.

"Oh." I cleared my throat, a little embarrassed by my mistake. "She's very wise and nice," I said. "She cares deeply about everyone and everything in Aventurine."

"This is very good to know." The mayor smiled and sighed, as though a great concern had been put to rest.

"Tell us about your mission," Jango said.

Queen Patchouli hadn't sworn me to secrecy, but I was vague anyway. I didn't want to risk word of the new baby queen reaching less-benevolent ears.

"I have to get something that belongs to her," I said, "from the cloud people."

Everyone who heard me was suddenly silent.

Jango looked stricken. "You must not go to the Cantigo Uplands, Trinity. It is *dangerous*!"

"More than going below to find precious things," Targa said. "The cloud people hate outsiders."

"They do terrible things to intruders," Jango said. "Nobody goes there."

"And comes back," Targa added.

"I have to," I said. "Queen Patchouli chose me for this quest. But don't worry: I'll be in and out before the cloud people even know I'm there."

Mayor Mordo nodded. "We will very much hope for this, too."

I hadn't meant to throw a damper on the party and quickly changed the subject. "Would it be impolite or greedy to have a third biggle berry tart?"

"Oh, my, no!" The mayor erupted in a rumbling belly laugh. "Berto will be thrilled."

"He'll brag about it forever," Targa said.

I spent the rest of the night sipping cider, listening to funny stories, and dancing. The Curipoo love to sing boisterous songs and howl. They're extremely energetic, and their dances look like a cross between Irish jigs and American square dancing.

I showed them how to do the Haka, a Maori war

dance that involves a lot of slapping the chest, stamping feet, popping eyes, and sticking out your tongue. It's supposed to psych a warrior up to fight and scare the enemy. The Curipoo thought it was funny.

Full of good food and exhausted, I slept soundly until I was jolted awake by another flying-crashing dream. This time, I was riding a Maori kite that spiraled out of control when it lost lift.

I finished a breakfast of nuts, warm honey bread, and biggle berry tarts just before Jango and Targa arrived. They were, as they put it, happy sad.

"We want to see your kite!" Jango exclaimed.

"But we don't want you to go," Targa said. "You *have* been the best guest ever, and we don't want anything very bad to happen to you."

I didn't want them to worry, so I made light of what might lie ahead. "I'll be fine. Queen Patchouli gave me everything I need to succeed. She expects me to return to the Willowood, and I wouldn't dare disappoint her."

They both brightened instantly, and there was a distinct bounce in their step when we went back to the shops we had passed yesterday. They would not argue with the great Queen Patchouli's wisdom.

In the first shop, I found thin supple branches, dry grasses, flat vines, and flaxlike flowers that would make an excellent Maori kite. But before I left with my supplies, I picked up a length of silky material.

"What is this?" I asked Targa and Jango.

"The top layer of tree bark," Targa said.

"We peel off what we need," Jango explained. "Then the tree grows a new layer."

"Perfect!" I added the material to my stash.

I wanted to pay, but I didn't have anything to offer. After Jango explained the human custom of buy-and-trade, the shopkeeper assured me that my comical dancing the night before was payment enough.

Jango, Targa, and I found a flat space where the morning sun shone through the leaves. I set down my kite-making materials and went to work. The Curipoo watched intently as I formed a basic American kite cross with two branches. Instead of the usual diamond shape, however, I made the sides longer than the vertical so the kite looked more like it had wings. Wrapping the middle with vine, I tightened it to hold the cross branches in place.

"Two sticks can't fly," Jango said.

Targa poked him in the ribs.

I was careful not to look insulted. Jango wasn't trying to be mean.

After I notched the ends of the cross sticks, I measured the size and shape of the silky bark that I needed and used Targa's carving tool to cut it. Next,

I cut slits for the notches and fitted the fabric so that it was pulled tight across the frame. Finally, I took the spool of unbreakable string out of my backpack and tied it to the middle cross section.

"That's it?" Jango asked. "You're done?"

I frowned and rubbed my chin. Something was missing. A Maori kite wasn't done until it was adorned with dried flowers, ribbons, or shells. But I wasn't sure how to add them to the silky fabric.

"It still needs decoration," I said.

Targa perked up. "Try placing your flowers where you want them," she suggested.

That seemed like a reasonable place to start. With Jango and Targa's help, I placed the flowers on the fabric in a pretty arrangement. When I placed the last flower, I gasped. The flowers that had been placed first were melting into the fabric.

Targa and Jango both laughed. "The bark fabric loves to soak up flowers. That's one of the ways our clothes get such great color," said Jango.

"How do you keep it from sucking up all sorts of colors?" I was intrigued.

Jango scooped up some dirt from the floor and held

out his paw. "Just blow this dust on it. For some reason, the dust sets the colors permanently."

The flowers had all melted away, and my kite was now a rainbow of bright colors. I took some dust from Jango's paw and blew it over the kite. The dust shimmered briefly and then disappeared.

"Okay, I guess we're done!" I stood up and held the kite high. "Now let's see if it flies."

The Curipoo led me to a wide space on the edge of the limb. A strong breeze circled us. They gasped when I dropped the kite and cheered when it lifted higher and higher into the air, pulling the string through my fingers. Using tactics I had mastered long ago, I dazzled them with my fairy kite's dips and loops.

Jango clearly wanted to try it, but I could tell he wasn't sure if it was proper to ask. Keeping my hand safely on the spool, I placed his hand on the string.

"Oh, no!" Jango's eyes bulged, but he held on tight. "What if I break it?"

"You won't," I said. "You're a natural. I can tell."

Targa nodded her encouragement.

"Feel the kite through the string," I said. "When it starts to dip, pull back. When it pulls, let it out."

We flew the kite for an hour or so. Then I felt it was time for me to leave.

Targa threw her arms around my legs and hugged. "We'll miss you."

"And I'll miss you," I said. "But I'll remember you whenever I look at your beautiful flower bead, and you'll remember me when you and Jango make and fly kites."

"It's okay for us to make kites like yours?" Jango asked, stunned.

"Of course," I said. "Someday, when I return, the sky will be full of Jango's and Targa's kites!"

"Yes!" Jango jiggled with joy. "We will give them to everyone!"

"And I bet you'll come up with some fantastic designs of your own, too," I added. I could almost see the wheels start to spin in Targa's creative head.

I wanted to stay longer, but my quest was too important to put off. I put the spool of string in my pack and fastened the kite to my harness. Then, with Jango and Targa at my side, we headed back toward the tree trunk. Mayor Mordo, Berto, Jobri, and many other Curipoo were waiting by the Great Hall to see me off.

Mayor Mordo handed me a silk bark sack. "Some bread and fruit for your journey," he explained.

"And four biggle berry tarts!" Berto shouted. "I made them fresh this morning."

"Thank you so very much," I said. "Do the steps go all the way to the top of the tree?"

"No," Jango answered. "They stop here."

"We don't go higher unless it's very necessary," the mayor added. "Those who dwell in the forest above do not bother us, and we do not bother them."

With luck, they would not bother me, either.

"No one has to cross our branch to travel up or down," Jango said.

"The tree is large," Targa added, "with many branches on the far sides."

It was good to know I didn't have to worry about other beings until I reached the upper branches, which—when I looked up—seemed impossible. The next limb was twenty-five feet higher with nothing but open space in between.

Jango read my mind. "We have a way, Trinity."

"But it's not very safe," Targa said. "We only use the fling-vine in emergencies."

Fling-vine? I blinked as I pictured myself being catapulted to the next branch.

My mental image seemed far-fetched but was uncomfortably close to reality.

The fling-vine was a heavy rope looped over a limb at least fifty feet above. One end was attached to a huge boulder perched on the edge of the Curipoo limb. I could see where this was going.

"You're sure about this?" I asked, looking to Targa and Jango.

"We have stories of it working in the past," said Jango.

"The past? How 'past' are we talking about here?"

"Um, I'm sure you'll be fine. Just put your foot in this toe-loop thing and hold on really tight," said Jango.

With that not-so-reassuring response, I slipped one foot into the toe-loop and held on with both hands.

The Curipoo crowd waved good-bye.

I bid them a Kiwi farewell. "Cheerio!"

Then three large Curipoo pushed the boulder off the tree.

6

Fall or Fly

I squealed as I was jerked off the branch.

Bark, leaves, and vines blurred past me in a whoosh. Suddenly, I arrived at the branch that I was trying to reach, but instead of stopping, the kite in the harness on my back shot me higher into the sky.

I felt like I was truly flying. It was a mixture of terror and joy. But, like my dream, I knew the flight would end in disaster. The third branch was too high, and there was no way I could reach it.

Still hurtling upward, I scanned the space above and saw that vines streamed off the next limb.

Out of reach.

In the same instant, I felt my speed begin to stall. Desperate and determined, I stretched, willing myself to stay aloft just long enough to capture a hopefully strong vine. My heart leaped into my throat when my hand closed around a woody tendril. It didn't break. Without pausing to think, I climbed hand over hand to the limb and collapsed in a tangle of vines.

Stunned by the unexpected good luck, I huddled in my impromptu nest, struggling to catch my breath and savoring the feeling of just being alive.

Mostly I thought about the few fabulous seconds I had spent flying. The sensation had been an illusion, but it had still been the most amazing experience I'd ever had.

My fairy kite had made all the difference. A heavier Maori kite would not have carried me so far, and like the legendary Tawhaki, who fell when his kite was attacked by a bird, I would have crashed.

At least, that's how a twentieth-century version of the Tawhaki legend went. I preferred the older, *Arawa* myth.

I thought about Tawhaki's story and how his journey was a bit like mine so far.

After Tawhaki insulted his infant daughter, his wife took the baby and vanished into the sky. Intent on getting them back, Tawhaki and his younger brother tried to climb to them on vines. The brother fell to his death when the wind whipped the hanging vine he chose to climb. Tawhaki used the sturdy parent vine and reached the tenth heaven, where he learned many spells and was reunited with his wife and child.

A sturdy vine had saved me from a fatal fall, and I was climbing into the sky to save a baby. Not to mention that the tree was so big and the Cantigo Uplands seemed so far, I'd feel like I had climbed ten heavens when I got there.

I paused long enough to sip water from my pod and eat one of Berto's biggle berry tarts. Then, taking care not to snag my kite, I pushed through the tangled vines, looking for an open space.

The Curipoo's branch had been pruned and cultivated to make space and let in sunlight. This branch was wild and untended. Dozens of different plants were bound together by curlicue tendrils of vine, forming thick ropes, mats, and misshapen ladders that connected this limb with a large branch above. Nothing else was visible within the thick greenery.

The distance between the third and fourth branches wasn't nearly as great as that between the first two limbs, and I reached the next branch in less than ten minutes. From there, I set a pace and climbed mechanically. The steady climbing was soothing, but sometimes I would zone out and forget to watch for danger.

A few branches up, I almost lost my footing when a slippery lavender tongue shot out of the leaves and curled around my wrist.

I gagged, but I kept Berto's tart in my stomach where it belonged.

I'm not usually squeamish about creepy-crawly things. Then again, I never imagined having a two-foot-long silver lizard with glistening black spots, four eyes, and ten legs dangling from my left arm. I tried to shake it off, but the stubborn creature wouldn't let go. I finally hooked my right arm around a thick vine, grabbed the lizard's body with my right hand, and unwound its tongue from around my wrist.

I set him down safely as far from me as possible. Then I scrambled like crazy to get away from it.

An hour later, I was swarmed by red tree frogs.

At first, I thought leaves were tickling my neck, but the tickling didn't stop when I tried to brush them away. I figured out what was happening when five tiny frogs landed on the back of my hand and began flicking their tongues to catch even tinier flies.

I shook my hand, but the tree frogs had suction-cup feet that stuck fast to my skin. Grimacing, I tried to pull one off. It stuck like ultra-glue, and I had to stop pulling before I hurt it or myself.

Something about me or my clothing was attracting the miniature flies, and the little frogs continued to swarm. Five became ten; ten became twenty; twenty became forty. At a loss, and with no way to fight, I did the only other thing I could think of.

I charged up a vine and climbed as fast as I could.

Slowly, the little frogs began to fall off. The farther away from their home I got, the fewer I had stuck to my skin and clothing. Eventually, I was frog-free.

I continued climbing, picking up speed as the foliage began to thin. Something about the frogs made me want to continue putting space between them and me.

Thankfully, the tree trunk protected me from the wind, and I did not meet any more Aventurine pests. But, when I paused to rest, the hairs rose on the back of my neck.

Is someone watching me?

Or stalking me for dinner?

Both prospects gave me the willies, and I tried to look casual. I used the excuse of drinking from my water pod to glance around. Surprise was my only advantage, and I didn't want the watcher to know I suspected him or her. I didn't see anyone, but that didn't put me at ease.

I had nowhere to hide.

Fighting the impulse to hurry, I calmly started upward again. I thought I heard a branch snap below, but no one was there when I looked down.

Then I heard whispers.

Or is it the wind?

The sound stopped when I stopped.

Much as I hated to admit it, the Curipoo's warnings about other, less friendly beings on the tree had made me a little nervous. Still, refusing to be bullied by my own fears, I kept climbing.

Leaves rustled.

A twig cracked.

And a monster grabbed me from above.

"Wha—" I gasped as thick aloe-like leaves whipped around my arms, legs, neck, and waist. My hands gripped the leaves clamped around my neck and pulled to loosen the hold just as I was yanked onto the next major limb.

My knees buckled when my shoes touched solid bark, but the leaves kept me upright. I had to keep pulling on the one around my neck to avoid being choked.

My captor stood out against the blood-black leaves that covered the limb. It was a mass of writhing leaf tentacles, kind of like the many-headed Hydra in ancient Greek mythology.

"Let me go!" I demanded.

The plant's iron grip tightened further when I struggled.

Furious and terrified, I imagined a future traveler finding my imprisoned skeleton and quickly rejected the very idea. I wasn't sure I'd survive my mission, but a stupid plant was *not* going to strangle me.

"Okay, let's try this." I exhaled and went limp, hoping the plant would *think* I died and retract its leaves.

Big mistake.

Apparently, the Hydra would not let anything go—dead or alive. When it sensed space between its tentacle leaves and my body, it squeezed. The tightening happened so fast I suddenly couldn't draw air.

Right when I thought I might pass out, an old man emerged from the tree trunk. *Like a ghost walking through a wall,* I thought.

His long white hair and beard were matted with forest debris and infested with bugs and small wiggly worms. Ribbons of blood-black slime shimmered in his tattered brown robe, and black snakes slithered around his feet. He carried a crooked wooden staff, and when he snapped his bony fingers, the plant released me.

I sank into a heap, gasping for air.

The old man glared at me with watery black eyes. He made no move to help.

"Who are you?" I asked in a harsh whisper.

"Hoon, Keeper of the Cloud Pine Forest," he growled.

"I'm Trinity—"

"I know who you are. You're a meddling fairy-godmother-in-training." Hoon spit out the words as though the sound left a sour taste in his mouth.

"Is that a problem?" I asked, buying time to gather my wits and regain my strength.

"A problem for you," Hoon said. "I do not like intruders, and I especially do not like little girls who come to Aventurine to *fix* things." He leaned close and snorted in my face. "I hate change."

I gagged on the stench of his foul breath and squirmed under his hateful stare. I didn't know what he wanted, but one thing was certain: I could not reveal that a new queen and great change were imminent in the fairy world. The Keeper would not welcome the news, and he certainly wouldn't help the girl Queen Patchouli had sent to make sure it happened.

"What are you doing here?" Hoon asked.

"Climbing a tree," I said.

"I know that!" the old man snarled. "Why?"

"Because it's the biggest tree I've ever seen," I said.

"That's a ridiculous reason," Hoon said.

More whispers rippled through the leaves, and from the corner of my eye I caught a glimpse of two other wrinkled men. Short and round with mottled gray skin, brown shirts, and white tufts of hair on speckled bald heads, they looked like toads. Their black eyes glittered with evil glee when they chuckled.

"But it doesn't matter why you're here," Hoon continued. "This is my branch, and you're not staying."

"That's right, I'm not." I stumbled to my feet and brushed dried leaves off my clothes. I couldn't wait to put the creepy old guy and his roly-poly gigglers behind me. "So if you'll excuse me, I'll be on my way."

I reached for a vine. Hoon waved his hand, and it snapped off in my hand.

"You're leaving the tree," the Keeper said, "as quickly as possible."

"Walk off!" A wrinkly little toad-man jumped out of the brush. His legs were so short he looked like a ball resting on two frog feet. "Walk off!"

Several other round men stepped out of the brambles and surrounded me.

"Walk off! Walk off!" they chanted.

"What's a *walk off*?" I had a good idea, but I had to know for sure.

"The quickest way to leave the tree is to walk off it." Hoon's upper lip curled into a sneer.

I gasped. "But I'll die!"

A toad-man looked up at me and grinned. "Walk off, fall down, die."

"Yes," Hoon agreed, "unless you're a true creature of the Cloud Pine Forest, like the Curipoo and black-spot lizards and a thousand other tree-dwelling beings and beasties. Then you'll survive."

The lizard and the Curipoo were creatures of the Cloud Pine Forest, but they couldn't fly. So they'd flunk Hoon's tree test, too. But at the moment, I didn't think logic was going to convince Hoon that his test didn't make sense. I quickly realized that I didn't have many options. Those I had weren't very good, but I had to try.

"I'd like to eat a last meal first," I told Hoon.

My plan was simple: Perhaps my captors would get bored waiting for me to finish the never-gone sweet potato and fall asleep. Then I could escape up the tree.

Hoon, however, was too anxious to kill me to grant a last request. "No."

With plan A down the gurgler, I moved on to plan B: If I anchored the unbreakable string, it might act like a bungee when I fell. Then I could grab a lower branch and find another way up the tree.

I shifted the harness and reached for the spool.

The Hydra slapped my hand away and tried to pull the harness off.

"No, please! Let me keep it. A harness pack is the most prized possession of my people," I lied. "If I'm going to die, I want to die with my pack on, like a real . . . cowboy."

I knew American cowboys liked to die wearing

some kind of gear—boots or a hat? I wasn't sure what, but the Keeper of the Cloud Pine Forest didn't know, either.

"What do you carry in there?" Hoon asked suspiciously.

"Food, a water pod, and string," I answered honestly. I touched the kite. "Uh . . . a Curipoo gave me this."

"Top bark and sticks?" Hoon scowled, then snorted. "Keep it all! You'll be heavier and will fall faster."

Again, I decided not to reason with him. Although I was dying to say that weight had nothing to do with how fast things fall, only wind resistance and an object's aerodynamics could slow it.

He brushed past me and stopped a few feet farther on. He waited with his back turned, expecting everyone to follow.

A toad-man poked me with a giant thorn. "Walk now!"

The others raised thorns to jab me if I didn't obey. I walked.

Hoon led the way down the branch, using his staff as a walking stick.

A well-worn path cut through the jungle of black vines and twisted tree branches. As the old man's minions herded me along, I wondered how many other unsuspecting travelers had been shoved off the branch. The toads were so excited about my imminent plunge to certain death that I was pretty sure it didn't happen often. Still, the thought made me angry, and my mind went into overdrive. I was still alive, and as my American friends liked to say, "Where there's a will, there's a way."

I had the will and another idea. Although plan C was based on science, not magic, it still required a leap of faith on my part. If I was right, I would live.

If not—

"Halt!" Hoon stopped and spun around to face me.

Beyond him, I could see a secondary branch that grew straight out from the main limb. It was about three feet wide, six feet long, and smooth as a board on top.

Like a plank on a pirate ship, I thought, but with one significant difference. If I walked the plank on a ship, I'd land in water. The ground below this plank was hard and a long, long way down.

"You wait!" one of the round men snapped as all the little guys closed in.

Hoon raised his staff and spoke in a booming voice. "We come to cast out one who is not of the Tree!" He fixed me with a cold stare. "Or to prove she belongs."

"No tree she!" a toad-man yelled.

"No tree she!" the others chanted. "No tree she!"

"I have permission! Queen Patchouli sent me to climb the tree." The partial truth was a gamble, but it was worth a shot.

"Did she now," the old man sneered. "Why?"

I lied again, hoping he respected Queen Patchouli's authority like the Curipoo. "I'm, uh . . . on a goodwill mission—like an ambassador."

"Intruders are *no* good!" Hoon exclaimed. "The punishment for trespassing is as it always has been and will be forever and ever. The prisoner will walk off—now!"

The round man to my left waved his thorn and shouted, "You walk off!"

Two more waddling toads stepped out of the bushes. One held a round drum under his chubby arm and beat it with a stick. The second guy blew an ear-piercing whistle every few beats.

"Walk!" Hoon ordered. He pounded the ground with his staff, keeping time with the drum.

I dug in my heels, but the little men pushed and prodded me with thorns until I was on the plank branch.

"All right!" I shouted, and held up my hands.

The despicable toad-guys stopped—just short of stepping onto the branch with me.

That's one thing in my favor, I thought. They were

afraid to walk out on the branch. I wasn't sure plan C would work, but it had a better chance if I was on the plank alone.

"Stalling won't save you," Hoon said.

"I'm not asking to be saved," I said. "I just want to die a warrior's death—bravely with a few final words to my ancestors." I didn't flinch as I met his black gaze. "Without being pushed."

"I will not deny you that," Hoon said, "just hurry up about it."

I pulled the Ananya talisman out from under my tunic and opened the top. I needed information, but I didn't want the horrible old man to suspect my intentions. I composed a chant off the top of my head.

"This Ananya daughter must ride the sky!" I moved farther out onto the branch and spoke as though I were imploring the spirits of my family. "Please take me swiftly and lift me up, whichever way the wind blows!"

The inside of the pendant mechanism clouded and then coalesced into a diagram. The image was similar in style to the hologram over Queen Patchouli's stone table, and the meaning was clear: The wind was moderately strong and blowing *away* from the tree.

"Enough!" Hoon glared at me. "Walk off now!"

"As you wish." I grabbed my kite, ran to the end of the plank, and jumped off the branch.

7

Moa

I dropped like a rock.

The toads laughed and chanted. "Walk off! Fall down! Walk off! Fall down!"

For a terrifying moment, I thought I had horribly miscalculated everything: wind speed, my kite's lift, and a not-quite-but-almost belief that I could fly.

"You dead now!" a little man yelled.

The others chimed in. "Dead now! Dead now!"

Not dead yet, I thought. As the bottom fell out of my stomach, I reached for the sky and angled the kite to catch a current of air.

The silky bark fluttered and then stretched taut in a sudden updraft. I laughed as the kite rose higher and flew past the astonished little men on Hoon's branch.

"Fly away!" The toads bounced and clapped,

enjoying my flight to safety as much as they had anticipated my demise. "Fly away!"

"No fair!" Hoon stamped his feet and shook his staff. "Fairy godmother brats can't fly!"

This one can, I thought, *when the wind and the kite are strong.*

So far I had climbed straight up from branch to branch in a vertical line. However, the giant tree was round with limbs on all sides. They were just spaced too far apart on the massive lower trunk to see. The major limbs were closer together now, and the wind carried me out and away from the Keeper's branch to the next one up and over.

I quickly learned a basic method of steering and aimed for the middle of the limb. Just before I reached it, I flipped the top end of the kite toward me and pushed in on the flap end. That slowed me enough to touch down. I stumbled forward, grabbed a smaller branch, and jerked myself to a stop.

The plants on the new branch were similar to the thorn thickets and blood-black leaves on Hoon's branch, but not as gruesome. The vines were green and supple and the leaves were red with green veins. I didn't see any menacing Hydra plants or nasty little toad-guys, but I was wary and watchful as I made my way across the limb.

The flight from Hoon's branch had been quick and easy compared to the climb. If I could do it again, I'd save time and energy. I stood on the edge of the branch with a clear view of the next branch higher up and over on the trunk. Leaving nothing to chance, I opened my compass and checked conditions again. They were exactly the same. I raised the kite and flung myself into the sky with the boldness of an eagle. The kite instantly caught the wind.

I continued flying from branch to branch on a route that spiraled up and around the tree. The distance was greater, but I traveled much faster. I also got lazy and overconfident as the afternoon wore on and the mechanics became routine. I didn't realize that the major limbs were growing closer and closer together until a small branch caught the side tip of my kite and pulled the silky bark out of the notch.

I lost my balance, tumbled onto the rough bark, and rolled to a stop.

Alarmed by my loud, undignified entrance, a round, fuzzy yellow creature with fangs scolded me from the side of the tree trunk. Two other vampire tennis balls tried to hoist the fallen kite into a hollowed-out gnarl.

"That's mine!" I got to my feet and rolled up the unbreakable string as I moved toward the kite.

The yellow creatures hissed and shrieked, but when I got too close, they dropped their prize and fled into their hole.

The damage to the kite was minimal, and I quickly made repairs. Then I attached it to my harness. The branches above were even closer together, and I didn't want the kite to get tangled and broken. Flying was more efficient and fun, but I still liked climbing trees the old-fashioned way.

The vines and other plants had thinned out, giving the tree's offshoot branches room to grow. There were plenty of places to hold on, and I had no trouble maintaining a brisk pace. I didn't know how high I had come, but it had to be at least a mile.

The life-forms on the higher branches were just as awesome and diverse as those on the superhuge limbs below. I climbed through a cloud of blue butterflies that jangled like bells, I shed tears when a fungus-clam spit onion juice in my face, and I gagged when my hand sank into a mushy melon plant. The melon closed around my arm and sucked it in past my elbow. I pulled free, but the mush on my skin hardened like cement and smelled like turpentine mixed with rotten tomatoes.

As though Aventurine decided I deserved a break, I found a natural spa on the next branch.

I stood for a minute, surveying the surroundings

and hoping my mind wasn't playing tricks. Logically, the lush gardens and gurgling hot springs couldn't possibly exist in the top of a tree.

But this was a fairy world, and anything was possible. Adorable puppy creatures and grumpy toadmen had proven that.

I still didn't move, wondering if there was a catch.

Giant ferns and multicolored flowers grew around the tiered rock walls that formed several pools.

I moved slowly toward one of the smaller pools. I desperately needed to wash off the melon mush crust on my arm. My presence didn't seem to bother the furry otterlike creatures that dove playfully in the water. Either they didn't notice me or they didn't feel threatened.

I paused at the edge of the pool. The water was so clear I could see the bottom. The pool wasn't deep, and nothing swam, crawled, or walked on the smooth rock floor.

I put my hand in to test the water temperature and sighed. It was hot but not boiling—like a bath made for soothing sore muscles.

"Is it all right if I take a bath?" I asked no one in particular.

When no response came, I stripped off my harness and clothing and slipped into the water.

The warm spring began to bubble, and I stretched

out with a contented sigh. The hardened mush and other debris I had collected in my hair were washed away, and the heat eased the tightness in my muscles. Using a lily pad as a washcloth, I carefully cleaned a few scratches and scrapes. Then I languished in the soothing bath until I caught myself dozing off.

When I finally made myself get out, I realized that I didn't have a towel, but the moisture on my skin evaporated quickly in a light breeze. I dressed, ate the rest of my Curipoo food, drank some water, and fell asleep under a canopy of ferns just as the light faded from the sky.

It was still dark when I woke up.

Stiff from sleeping on the ground, I sat up slowly. My hat, backpack, kite, and harness were all in a neat pile by my side, right where I had left them. I drank some water and ate as much never-gone sweet potato as I could stomach. I didn't know how much farther I had to go to reach the Cantigo Uplands, but I was pretty sure I wouldn't be fed when I got there.

When I saw light through leaves, I strapped on my harness, made my way back to the trunk, and started climbing again.

Half an hour later, I began to feel uneasy. Thirty feet farther up, goose bumps rose on my arms and my heart began to beat faster. It wasn't based on evidence of any kind. I just had a feeling that something terrible lay ahead. Premonitions defied logic, and I usually rejected such things as ridiculous hysteria. However, with Hoon's attempt to kill me fresh in my mind, I decided to err on the side of caution.

I slowed my pace and moved forward on high alert.

The higher I climbed, the more intense the feeling of dread became. On edge and wary, I paused when I noticed swirls of black mist above me. Thick and opaque, it covered the entire length of the next branch, obscuring everything.

The danger was definitely there.

But I couldn't turn back. And yet, I couldn't charge ahead, either. Climbing as quietly as possible, I entered the mist and paused to get my bearings. The interior of the cloud wasn't as dark or dense as it appeared from the outside. I could see through the haze. I just couldn't make out many details.

My ears, however, worked perfectly, and I was drawn to the sound of distressed squawks, chirps, hoots, and screeches.

Determined not to be captured again, I crept from one gnarl in the branch to another. Most of the non-tree vegetation was dead or dying. I wanted to avoid whatever sinister being was in control here, but I couldn't ignore the sound of cries for help.

The noise was coming from a clearing filled with the stumps of large chopped-off branches. I crouched to avoid being seen and peered through the mist. Birds of all sizes and descriptions were locked in cages that hung from branches or were stacked on the ground. Some of the prisoners were shackled and chained to stumps. Dented water buckets and rusted feed pans were scattered around, none within reach of the captives. Their misery and fear was so great I could feel the weight of it in my heart.

I couldn't leave the birds here to suffer.

But I couldn't act until I knew the enemy.

I didn't have to wait long.

A woman emerged from the mist, pulling a wagon topped with a cage. She walked stooped over with a slow, shuffling gait and used a crooked cane. Her gray hair was tangled, and her black dress was tattered and patched. She was so thin she looked like a skeleton covered in wrinkled, gray skin. I didn't realize what she was until she turned to hit one of the hanging cages with her cane. Blackened wings hung limply on her hunched back.

The woman was a fairy!

110

"Stop whining, you stupid bird!" The dark fairy's voice cracked, and she smacked the cage again. "You should thank me for feeding you."

The bird in the hanging cage appeared weak from hunger, but it squawked in brave defiance. "I only pity you, Kasandria. You'll never fly again."

"You won't, either!" Kasandria hit the cage repeatedly, sending a flurry of red and black feathers flying everywhere. Then, her anger and energy spent, she pulled the wagon into the center of the clearing and stopped.

For a moment, I thought the bird in the cage had keeled over and died. I was relieved when it climbed back onto its perch.

"Look at me, lazy birds!" Kasandria screamed. "I have a new pet!"

A few of the birds looked up. Most cowered in their cages or hid behind stumps. The mound of blue and gray feathers in the wagon cage didn't move when Kasandria opened the door. She clamped a shackle and chain around the bird's leg and pulled it out.

"Don't be shy." The evil fairy cackled and thumped the bird on the back when it tried to hide its head.

I couldn't believe my eyes. The new bird looked like a moa, though its neck and legs were too short and it only stood three feet tall. Wingless, the huge New Zealand moa had been hunted to extinction by the Maori hundreds of years ago. Judging by its size, this one was only half-grown.

"Now fly, Moa!" Kasandria demanded.

"I can't," Moa said.

"Of course you can!" The fairy glowered at the poor creature. "You're a bird."

"I don't have wings," the bird explained.

Kasandria hesitated, as though Moa's statement was too incredible to believe. When she stepped closer and ran her hands over the bird's body, she discovered that he really didn't have wings.

"I want birds that can fly!" Enraged, Kasandria swung her cane at Moa's head. He ducked, and she missed. "So I can make sure that they *don't*!"

Moa tried to run.

Kasandria grabbed the end of his chain, looped it through another bird's cage, and secured it with the lock from the wagon.

Then she went berserk.

"Queen Patchouli did this!" Kasandria chased a round, white chicken and then smashed a lantern. She tore vines and dumped feed pans. "She made a bird with no wings to taunt me! I won't have it!"

The birds panicked and shrieked as Kasandria

rattled cages, pounded stumps, and threatened to barbeque, fry, and roast every last one.

Moa was shaking so hard some of his feathers fell out, but he found the courage to speak up. "It wasn't Queen Patchouli."

The fairy turned, stomped toward the terrified bird, and hovered over him. "Who else wants me to pay more than I already have for trying to be the best fairy flier in Aventurine?"

Why is that a crime? I wondered.

Moa asked, "Is that wrong?"

"It is if you cast a grounding spell on the mushroom stew so your clan sisters can't fly." Kasandria's eyes narrowed. "Queen Patchouli stripped me of my fairy powers and banished me. If she didn't create you to mock me, who did?"

"I dared to suggest that cloud people and fairies could be friends," Moa said. "As punishment, King Shyne turned me into a bird with no wings and ordered his guards to drop me here."

"To ridicule me!" Kasandria shook her cane at the big bird. "If I had the power, I'd turn you into a dragon and send you back to evaporate all those high-and-mighty mist people with your fiery breath. Since I can't do that, I'll kill you instead—as soon as I find my knife."

"No, please!" Moa backed to the length of his chain.

Several of the other birds gasped. I waited and watched as Kasandria began a frantic search for her misplaced blade. She looked under cages and dumped seed out of food dishes. She even checked in tangles of dead vines and inside hollow gnarls. Kasandria tore through the clearing like a tornado, smashing anything that got in her way.

Birds crawled out of broken cages and hid. Some hungrily pecked at the spilled seed on the ground. Those who were chained jumped and dodged to avoid Kasandria's thrashing cane. Her destructive tantrum ended as quickly as it began when the fairy decided that her knife wasn't in the clearing.

"It must be in my house," Kasandria muttered as she headed back into the mist.

I crept out of hiding and started to follow. I knew that I couldn't let her find her knife and kill the moa. But I didn't have any kind of weapon to stop her.

I pulled my still-damp hair back behind my ears to see better, and my hand brushed the feather that Queen Patchouli had given me. Maybe it was a weapon. I carefully unwound the feather from my hair.

Disappointment sat like a stone in my gut. The feather's end wasn't sharp; it was rounded and had nubs along the edge. In fact, it looked a lot like a key.

"It will be quite useful under certain circumstances," Queen Patchouli had said.

With the feather clutched in one hand, I darted to the nearest cage. The vulture inside started to speak.

I put my finger to my lips and shook my head. "Don't make a sound until I give the signal," I whispered. "I want to free everyone before Kasandria returns."

The bird nodded and watched as I slipped the quill into the lock. The feather quivered in my hand. Then the lock clicked and opened. I removed it and moved on to the cage with the red and black bird Kasandria had terrorized. The feather morphed into a perfect key to fit that lock, too.

"Are you strong enough to fly?" I asked softly. When the bird nodded, I told it to wait for my signal.

I quickly unlocked all the cages and then moved on to the chained birds. I freed the moa first.

"Who are you?" the big bird asked.

"Shhh!" I took the shackle off and clamped my hand around the bird's beak. "Be quiet until I tell you to fly," I whispered.

"Uh can't fuh," the bird mumbled through its closed beak.

"Then run for the trunk," I said.

He nodded and fluffed his feathers. "Uh can wun wally fas."

"Shhh!" I shook my head as I moved on to the little white chicken.

The chicken squatted to wait and didn't make a peep. The other birds, including the moa, were so still the clearing seemed eerily quiet. They didn't move until Kasandria came shuffling out of the mist, walking with her cane and waving a knife.

"Nobody makes a fool out of me," the fairy said.

"Fly now!" I shouted.

The stronger birds rose into the air and flew straight at the startled fairy. The moa, the white chicken, and several others ran toward her on foot. All of them screeched and squawked as they attacked.

"How did you get loose?" Kasandria swung her knife and cane as several hunting birds dove to rake her with their talons. "Get away! Shoo!"

I had freed the birds so they could escape. But it seemed they wanted Kasandria to pay for mistreating them first.

The moa and the grounded birds charged. As Kasandria backed away, other birds bombed her with twigs and nuts. The hunters continued their assault, driving the horrid fairy into the mist and past a ramshackle house.

Kasandria gave up trying to fight off the attack and tried to find cover under vines and behind ferns. The birds easily tore away the plants and forced her to keep moving. I followed the trail through crushed vines and broken branches until the moa and the other grounded birds stopped. When I came out of the mist, I saw that the birds had driven their tormentor to the edge of the branch.

"Go away, you stupid birds! I'll get you for this!" Kasandria tried to beat the attackers back, but they kept diving and pushing. She hooked her cane on an overhead branch and held on with both hands.

I ran forward, hoping to save the fairy, but I was too late. She stumbled and the birds made no move to help her. Her hands slipped from her cane, and she fell.

The fairy shrieked as she plummeted out of sight to her death.

The moa stepped up beside me. "She was very bad."

"Yes, she was," I agreed. Revenge was never the right solution, but somehow it was hard to blame the birds. They were free, but if Kasandria had lived, she would have captured and mistreated others.

As I walked back to the clearing, most of the birds flew away. The grounded birds decided to make the branch their own. With Kasandria gone, there was nothing to fear. They began by tearing down her house.

I headed back to the main trunk.

"Is that a flower?" the moa asked.

I didn't realize the big bird was following me until he spoke. I glanced at the vines overhead and smiled. Several flowers had bloomed, and new green growth was visible under the dead leaves. Moss appeared on the stumps and berry bushes sprouted through the ground bark. Free of the fairy's evil influence, the whole branch was coming back to life. The birds that chose to stay would not go hungry or want for fresh nesting materials.

"You'll have a nice home here . . . um . . . what's your name?" I asked.

"You can call me Moa. And what should I call you?"

"My name's Trinity."

"Brave Trinity, I owe you my life. I cannot stay here now. I have a debt to repay you. Until I save your life, I will be your companion," Moa said with a bow.

I stopped, and Moa plowed into me.

"Watch it," the bird said.

My temper flared. "You bumped into me!"

"You were in the way," Moa huffed.

"You can't come with me," I said. The last thing I needed on a quest to rescue a baby queen from hostile cloud people was an outcast mist person who was stuck in the body of a bird that couldn't fly.

"Yes, I can. I must," the bird insisted. "Cloud people never forsake a life-for-a-life obligation."

"I won't tell," I said.

"I'm staying," Moa countered.

"Okay, suit yourself." I was certain that the stubborn bird would change his mind. He couldn't fly, and he wasn't equipped to climb. Everything Moa needed to survive was on the branch. I wouldn't feel the least bit guilty leaving him behind.

"I can give you valuable information. Like, nothing hurts mist people," Moa said, "except maybe dragon fire. Any kind of intense heat, actually. If we explosively evaporate, like in an instant, our molecules don't always condense again. Then we're dead."

I took mental notes, but I didn't let him know I was paying attention.

"A lot of stuff hurts solid bodies," Moa said. "I guess that's why King Shyne chose this form to punish me. As a solid, I can't float on the wind or compress and compete in icicle tournaments or disperse so a wicked fairy's cane passes right through me."

"If the Cantigo Uplands are made of clouds, did you just fall through?" I asked, so I would know what to expect when I got there.

"No, the clouds adjust to support whatever weight is present," Moa explained. "I was lucky King Shyne and Queen Sonja didn't have me thrown off the Long-Way-Down Peninsula. Instead, they deliberately had me heaved onto Kasandria's branch."

"Did they want to make her mad?" I asked.

"No, they wanted me to see how terrible fairies are," Moa said.

"Kasandria was terrible," I explained, "but most fairies are go— *Hnk!*" I was jerked to a halt by a strong pull on my harness. I snapped my head around.

Moa's beak was clamped onto my harness straps. He spit them out.

"What was that for?" I asked.

"You almost stepped on that stinkbug," Moa said. "Bad for him if he dies. Bad for you if he sprays his stink. It's hard to hide if you smell really bad."

I looked down and saw a line of beetles walking across our path.

"Um, thanks. So, mist people can smell things?" I asked.

"Yes, we are beings of the air and very sensitive to scents," Moa said.

I added that information to my Cloud People Fact File.

When we reached the tree trunk, I didn't stop to say good-bye. I started climbing. When I was twenty feet higher, I paused to look back.

Moa wasn't stranded. He was ten feet behind me, scaling the tree using his beak and talons.

"Don't worry about me!" Moa gripped a branch

and the trunk bark with his talons and shouted, "I'll catch up!"

I couldn't make Moa go away, so I ignored him. That wasn't hard to do. He couldn't talk while he was using his beak to climb, and I had to concentrate on my foot- and handholds as we got closer to the top of the gigantic pine. The branches here were much thinner, and the narrowing trunk swayed in the wind.

Eventually, I paused in the crook of a sturdy branch. The tip-top of the tree was less than thirty feet away, and it wasn't safe to climb higher on the flimsy branches.

From this vantage point, I had a great view of the other trees in the Cloud Pine Forest. The giant pines stretched as far as I could see in three directions, and they were laced with clouds.

"That's where I come from." Moa gripped the tree with his talons and nodded to the left.

The cloud territory called the Cantigo Uplands hovered just off the side of the tree, forty or fifty feet up. The only way to reach it was by kite.

"You have to stay here, Moa," I said.

"I'd rather go back down with you," the bird said.

"I'm going to the Cantigo Uplands."

The bird blinked. "No."

"I'm on a mission for Queen Patchouli," I said.

"I have to rescue a fairy baby that's being born there."

"No," Moa insisted. "I have an obligation to keep you from harm. King Shyne has never dealt with an intruder, but King Whone before him turned an outsider into snowflakes and scattered him across the land. You can't go."

"I have to," I said. "It's a fairy-godmother-in-training obligation I can't refuse."

"Then I'm going with you." Moa grabbed my harness with a talon and then glanced at the cloud country. "Except I can't fly, so we can't get there anyway."

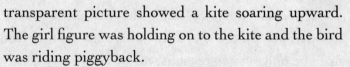

"I can fly—sort of." I just didn't know if my kite could carry Moa's extra weight. I pulled out my pendant and opened the compass. "Wind speed and kite lift for two?"

Moa peered over my shoulder as a fog covered the mechanism and cleared. The transparent picture showed a kite soaring upward. The girl figure was holding on to the kite and the bird was riding piggyback.

Moa gasped. "I don't know if that's a good idea. I'm supposed to protect you. Not let you fly into danger."

"I'm going with or without you," I said. "But I've got an idea to make it a little safer. Let go so I can work."

"Promise you won't leave me," the bird said.

"I won't leave you."

Moa nodded and moved to the branch below. I peeled off a long piece of the silky top layer of bark and fashioned it into a sling. Then I untied my kite and slipped the sling around my chest and one shoulder.

I called Moa back up to the branch. He understood the sling idea immediately and crawled into it so that he was pressed against my back. I made sure he held on to the harness with his talons. Then I positioned myself for takeoff.

"Ready?" I asked.

"We will fly or die together. It will be an honor," Moa said as he tightened his grip.

I took a deep breath and set my sights on the cloud domain. *Aotearoa,* the Maori name for New Zealand, means "long white cloud." *Maybe that's a good omen,* I thought as I launched us into the air.

8

Cloud Travel

I knew immediately that it would be difficult to steer. The high altitude meant sudden updrafts, down-drafts, and crosswinds. Not to mention that Moa was clinging stubbornly to me. I struggled to keep the kite level and on course.

"I feel sick," Moa moaned.

"Are you going to throw up?" I asked.

"No!" the bird huffed, insulted.

"Good!" I shot back.

The kite dipped steeply to one side, and Moa's talons dug into my back.

"Ouch!" I winced. "Don't do that!"

Moa sneezed.

Startled, I jerked and lost control.

"We're falling!" the bird cried out.

I angled the kite into a controlled dive, banked,

and got us heading upward again. Shaken, I focused on flying and our destination.

The mishap must have unnerved Moa, too. He didn't make another sound until we approached the cloud realm and I asked a question.

"Will someone see us coming?" I wanted to get in and out of the Cantigo Uplands without the cloud people knowing I had been there, just as I promised Jango and Targa.

"Only if someone is looking this way," Moa said.

"Do cloud people hang out on the edges?" I asked.

"Only those who think they can fall like rain and survive." Moa sighed. "A few have tried, but no one has ever returned."

I put that in my Cloud People Fact File, too. I could escape over the edge with my kite, and they would not pursue.

"Where's the best place to land?" I asked.

Moa turned his head toward the cloud. "There's one."

I looked at the wide indentation in the coastline as we sailed past. I didn't want to turn around. Flying with the wind was hard enough without trying to fly against it.

"I need more warning!" I yelled.

"Okay." Moa paused a second. "There's one. There's another one. That looks like a good spot."

"Does that mean I can land anywhere?" I asked.

"Almost anywhere," Moa said. "You don't want to land near a spoonga cave. They devour mist creatures." He made a slurping sound to demonstrate.

"We're not mist creatures," I said as I added another fact to my file. So far, I knew three things that harmed mist people: heat, falling like rain from the cloud domain, and being eaten by spoongas.

"Oh, right!" Moa bobbed his head and made a rumbling sound in his throat. He was laughing. "Then you can land anywhere except places where mist people go."

Moa's information was vague and not very helpful. I gave up asking for advice and scanned the cloud coast myself. When I saw another wide notch, I banked and headed in.

"Hang on," I told Moa as we entered the Cantigo Uplands. According to him, the cloud would adjust to support weight. When I touched down, my feet sank into the soft terrain, but I didn't have time to panic. They rose back up when the ground solidified underneath me.

Moa slid off my back and breathed in deeply. "It's good to be home, but I hope nobody sees me."

"Would they arrest you or something?" I adjusted my hat, stuffed the sling into my pack, and attached the kite to my harness.

"No, I've already been punished for believing that cloud people aren't superior to everyone else in Aventurine," Moa said. "Having the wits to escape the bird fairy and coming back isn't a crime, but I'm still solid, so I'm still an outcast."

"Unless the king decides to change you back," I said.

Moa gave me a long, beady-eyed stare. "I suppose that could happen—when he decides to be friends with fairies."

So you're stuck being solid, and I'm stuck with you, I thought as I glanced around to get my bearings. The cloudscape wasn't all white or gray as I expected but softly colored in pastels. It wasn't fluffy, either. We had landed among pointed pillars and craters made of hard foam.

"Where's the baby?" Moa asked.

"Huh?" I stared at him. Queen Patchouli hadn't told me where the new queen would be born. I assumed I would just find her somehow, like so many other inexplicable things that happened in Aventurine. "I don't know."

Moa blinked and stared back. "Trinity, I don't want to upset you, but what kind of plan is *that*?"

He was right. "It's not *my* plan," I said. "It's more like Queen Patchouli's plan."

"Why would the wise and wonderful Queen Patchouli send you to get something you can't find?" Moa asked.

"She wouldn't." I frowned, remembering something else Queen Patchouli had told me.

"Everything you need to bring the baby back to the Willowood . . . will be available."

I had something that would locate the infant queen, but what? I ran down the list of my possessions: water pod—no; sweet potato—no; unbreakable string—no; harness and pack—no; kite—maybe; clothes—no; necklace—

My pendant!

My mother had told me the Ananya pendant would calculate conditions when I learned to fly, but she had also called it a compass. I pulled the round disk out from under my tunic.

"What's that?" Moa asked.

"If we're lucky, it's a fairy baby GPS." I opened the disk and asked, "Where will the new Willowood fairy queen be born?"

The filaments glowed, the tiny mechanism whirred, and a map of the cloud domain appeared. Two red dots glowed on the border and a tiny golden speck pulsed in the middle.

"I think that's us." I pointed to the red dots and then to the blinking speck. I assumed it would glow steadily like our red dots when the new queen arrived. "And that's where the baby will be born."

"That's Castle City," Moa said softly.

I shrugged. "I still have to go."

"I know." Moa sighed. "Follow me."

The bird led me around the craters and paused by a curved path at the bottom of a steep hill. The path looked like a bobsled run.

"What's wrong?" I asked.

"A spoonga made this trail," Moa said. "They draw moisture up and absorb it as they move."

I scanned the trail ahead. There was no sign of a large slug creature. "We'll have to be careful."

Moa moved away from the spoonga path and started up the hill. His talons gripped the spongy surface, but my shoes kept slipping. I removed them and discovered that my toes gripped almost as well as the bird's feet. I put my shoes in my backpack.

At the top of the ridge, we looked down another slope into a valley strewn with giant heads of cauliflower.

"What are those?" I pointed.

"Trees," Moa said.

"How far is Castle City?" I asked.

"Two more hills and a rolling plain," Moa said.

"Will it take long to get there?" I asked.

"I'm not sure. I apologize, Trinity. Mist people can alter form depending on the terrain," Moa said. "Before King Shyne changed me, I could have spread myself thin and floated on the wind all the way. I've never traveled through the uplands as a solid."

"Well, then we'll just have to figure it out as we go." I had an idea. Taking the sling out of my pack, I smiled reassuringly at Moa. I laid the sling on the ground. I sat on the forward half and patted the material behind me. "Have a seat and get ready for the ride of your life."

Moa squatted behind me and gripped my harness straps with his beak.

I pulled the sling up like the rolled front of a toboggan and pushed with my free hand. The silky bark slid forward so fast Moa almost fell off.

"Yee-haw!" I yelled as we picked up speed.

Moa made choked gurgling noises in his throat as we careened down the slope. He couldn't let go of the straps to scream. When we reached the bottom, the sled carried us on across the valley floor.

"Lean left!" I shouted, and we leaned when we

sped toward the first cauliflower mound.

We zipped past the tree without hitting it.

"Right!" I yelled.

Moa leaned and we missed the next mound. We zigzagged through the cauliflower forest, slowly losing speed until we stopped at the base of the next slope.

Moa immediately rolled off.

"Are you okay?" I asked.

"That was great!" he said. "Let's hurry up the next hill so we can do it again."

"I second that," I said, grinning.

Once again, I let Moa lead. He knew the area and his experience was proving invaluable.

Moa looked back. "Don't step in the little holes." He lowered his head to show me a three-inch opening.

"What's inside them?" I asked.

"Tube flowers," he said. "They open, swallow whatever steps in them, and seal closed."

I studied the ground closely before every step. Being eaten by the cloud version of a Venus flytrap was the worst fate I could imagine. The flowers might take forever to digest their meals.

The ground was riddled with the flower holes, but they weren't the only danger. Two-thirds of the way up, the slope curled over like a huge Hawaiian wave.

"Can we go around?" I asked, even though the curled crest stretched as far as I could see in both directions.

"It'll be shorter if we go through," the bird said.

"Will the cloud let us do that?" I asked. "I mean, cloudy stuff hardens when it feels weight."

Moa made the laughing sound in his throat again.

I *hated* being laughed at.

"I'd rather use the tunnel," Moa said.

My cheeks burned red, but Moa didn't seem to notice my embarrassment. He stopped by a two-foot-wide slit at the base of the curl and kept talking.

"Tunnels are stable once the ice lattice forms," the bird explained. "But we have to run through it."

"What's in there?" I hadn't expected the terrain and creatures of the Cantigo Uplands to be just as hostile as the cloud people. From the ground, clouds looked so beautiful and harmless.

"The worms in the lattice are blind but very sensitive to motion," Moa said. "When something moves, they shoot icicle darts. The faster we go, the less likely we'll be hit."

I peered into the tunnel. The other end was a mere pinpoint of light in the darkness. I put my shoes back on just in case there were worms in the ground.

"The darts go right through a mist person," Moa continued, "but I think they would stick a solid."

I could deal with a little pain, but I did not want to be shot in the head. I pulled the silky sling out of my pack and tied it around Moa's head and neck like a scarf.

"The silky bark is tough," I explained. "It might at least slow them down." I untied my kite and held it over my head like an umbrella. "Ready?"

"Yes, but you go first," the bird said. "Your legs are longer and faster. If I went first, I would slow you down."

I started to argue but changed my mind. Moa was trying to protect me, and his logic was sound. More darts would hit me if I ran behind the slower bird.

Taking a deep breath, I entered the tunnel and ran as fast as I could for the opening ahead. Hundreds of darts whizzed through the air around me, buzzing like a swarm of angry bees. They bounced off my kite with the pitter-patter rhythm of a heavy rain. I winced and yelped when a few hit my arms and legs. They stung.

Behind me, Moa squealed a lot more often. I owed him for being willing to take the brunt of the attack.

My lungs were bursting when I stumbled through the tunnel exit. I stooped over to catch my breath, but

I resisted the urge to collapse on the ground. Darts were stuck all over me, and I didn't want to accidentally push them in any deeper. I pulled a dart out of my leg. The small wound felt like it was on fire, but I didn't flinch. When Moa ran out, I forced him to stay on his feet, too. His thick feathers had protected his body from the spines, but he had so many darts embedded in his legs that he looked like a cactus.

"I have to take the darts out before you lie down," I said.

"Good idea. Thank you, Trinity," he said, panting.

Moa stood very still while I plucked the darts out of his legs. He didn't whine or moan, but I could tell by his trembling that he could feel the fiery venom as well. When I finished, I praised him for his bravery and bit my lip as I pulled the rest of the darts out of my skin.

"I don't want to do that again," Moa said with a backward glance at the tunnel.

"But you want to slide again, right?" I fastened my kite to my harness and spread the silky sling on the ground again.

Moa hopped on behind me. "Let's go!"

As soon as I felt his beak close around my harness straps, I pushed off down the hill.

The second slope wasn't as steep or as long as the first, and the valley floor had fewer cauliflower trees.

The ride wasn't quite as exciting until Moa started yanking on the harness straps. He wanted to tell me something, but he didn't want to let go to talk. When I took a good look ahead, I understood why.

We were speeding right for a huge, pulsing marshmallow.

"Is that a spoonga?" I asked.

Moa frantically tugged on my harness, and I took that as a yes.

"Lean!" I screamed. The bird and I both leaned as far to the right as we could without falling off the sled.

The spoonga couldn't move fast enough to fully intercept us, but it was flattening so that it covered more ground. Odds were we wouldn't be able to avoid clipping it.

Moa was so scared I could feel him shaking, but he didn't let go.

"Pull your legs in and hang on tight!" Holding on to the toboggan roll with one hand, I reached for my kite with the other.

I calculated our speed, the distance to impact, the angle of incline, and the spoonga's slow reaction rate. When we made contact with the outer edge of the creature, it was shaped more like a melting scoop of ice cream. The silky bark protected us as it slid across the spoonga's porous skin, and the spoonga started shifting to engulf us.

As the sled's momentum propelled us up the slope, I counted down. "Three, two, one—blast off!"

I raised the kite, and we sailed into the air like a skier off a ski jump. The kite couldn't keep us airborne, but it provided enough lift to clear the spoonga and land a safe distance away. The sled continued sliding to the base of the next hill.

"Hah!" Moa jumped off the silky bark and strutted about with his feathers fluffed. "That was incredible!"

"It was kind of cool." I sounded casual, but I was just as exhilarated.

We paused to calm our racing hearts and then tackled the last hill with a shared sense of accomplishment. No dangerous cloud plants or animals got in our way this time, and I felt energized when we walked through a tall notch in the third ridge.

My euphoria evaporated as quickly as a mist in summer-morning sunlight.

We stood on the edge of a butte, surrounded by spires of hard foam-rock and angular treelike formations that reminded me of modern art sculptures. A rolling plain of shifting rainbow colors separated us from the new queen's birthplace in the city on the distant horizon.

"It will take days to cross that," I said.

"And there's no place for solids to hide," Moa added.

"I still have to go." I checked the compass. The baby's golden light was still blinking, but it was noticeably brighter. I was starting to worry we wouldn't arrive in time if we traveled by foot.

"I go where you go," Moa said, "but first, let's eat." The bird dropped his head and pulled a bunch of pink grass with his beak. After he swallowed, he sampled some nearby berries. Then he made a clucking sound with his tongue. "Those are so good!"

"You sound surprised." I sipped water from my pod.

"Mist people absorb liquids," Moa said. "We don't consume whole leaves and fruits—or drain animals like the spoongas. But these particular plants aren't actually from the Cantigo Uplands."

"How did they get here?" I asked.

"Seeds and spores drift in on the wind or drop from birds flying over," Moa explained. "Anything that starts growing here thrives." He took another mouthful.

"Save some for us!" a familiar voice shouted.

I looked up to see the red and black bird from Kasandria's branch perched on a tree branch.

"Hi!" I waved. "I'm so glad to see you!"

"Not as glad as I am to see you!" the bird exclaimed.

"Do you have a name?" I asked.

"I was called Sunset long ago," the bird said. "Before I left the jungle and was captured."

"That's a good name," I said.

Sunset raised his hooked beak and whistled. A flock of birds flew off the tall foam-rock towers, circled, and landed. They were the birds I had freed from the evil fairy.

"How many of Kasandria's prisoners are here?" I asked.

"Most of those who can fly," Sunset said. "We stopped to eat and rest before we head home. Cloud people can't catch birds."

"Unless they don't have wings," Moa said.

"Yes, that is unfortunate for you." Sunset nodded in sympathy, then turned back to me. "What are you doing here?"

"I was sent by Queen Patchouli to rescue a fairy baby in Castle City," I said.

"But the cloud people hate outsiders," Sunset squawked, "especially fairies."

"It's something I have to do . . . for the good of all in Aventurine."

"*If* you get there in time," Moa said.

A hawk flew down from a higher branch and perched beside Sunset. "What's the problem?"

"Castle City is too far and crossing the plain is too dangerous," Moa explained.

"Freeing us from Kasandria was dangerous," Sunset said.

The other birds stopped pecking at pink grass and bubble berries to hoot, screech, and chirp in agreement.

"It was the right thing to do," I said.

"And we owe you a great debt," Sunset said. "Which we can only partially repay by flying you to Castle City."

"Are you sure? I don't want to put you in more danger," I said.

"It is the least we can do," said Sunset.

The other birds fluffed feathers and flapped wings. They all wanted to help.

"We appreciate the offer, but aren't we too big to carry?" asked Moa.

"It'll work perfectly if I make harnesses that several birds can lift," I said, pulling out the spool of string.

"That thread doesn't look strong enough!" Moa exclaimed. "I'm supposed to be protecting you, you know."

"I know, but trust me, Moa," I said. "It's strong enough."

The birds ate and napped while I knotted the string into seat slings. Sunset's beak made excellent scissors, and I finished just before nightfall.

"Flying in the dark will be much safer," Sunset said as I stepped into my harness.

Both harnesses looked like park baby swings with twenty ropes attached. When Sunset asked for volunteers, more than forty birds wanted to make the trip. The extras decided to fly with us in case one of the lifting birds needed to be relieved.

Although I had complete faith in the string and the flock, I closed my eyes when I walked to the edge of the cliff.

"Here we go!" Sunset called out.

I opened my eyes just as Moa tucked his head into his feathers. Above me, twenty birds began flapping their wings. The strings drew taut as I was slowly lifted off the ground. My heart flip-flopped when the ridge fell away, but my spirits soared as we rose into the darkening sky.

The extra birds flew alongside Moa and me, perhaps so we wouldn't feel quite so alone. Unable to see the cloudscape below in the dark, I kept my gaze fastened on the faraway lights of Castle City.

When Sunset whistled, a pigeon broke away from my side. The pigeon flew back a moment later and asked, "Where do you want to be dropped off?"

"As far from the castle as possible," Moa answered.

I looked at my compass. As the miles slipped by, the image of the baby's birthplace became larger. The blinking speck was located in a park area near the castle.

"Name the baby's location," I said to it on a hunch.

Words written in elegant script appeared over the park area: *Morning Dew Garden.*

The pigeon relayed the message to Sunset.

Moa gasped. "No! That garden is part of the castle grounds. King Shyne's magic is very powerful, Trinity. I'm a mist person and look what he did to me! You're allied with Queen Patchouli and the fairies. Whatever he does to you will be much, much worse."

"The future of Aventurine will be worse if I don't bring the baby back to the Willowood," I said. "Nothing else is more important, not even me."

"You're more important to *me*!" Moa exclaimed.

I smiled. "If something happens and I can't complete the mission, promise you'll take the baby back to the Willowood for me."

"I'm a bird who can't fly," Moa protested.

"No, you're a mist person who's not a coward like the king," I said.

"King Shyne isn't afraid of anything," Moa insisted.

"That's not true," I said. "He thinks cloud people

are better than everyone else, and he won't toler-
ate strangers or change because his arrogant beliefs
might be proven wrong. In fact, they *would* be proven
wrong."

"Really?" Moa asked.

"You're much stronger and more secure than
other mist people, Moa—even as a bird who can't fly!
You've done some amazing things since we first met."

"I have, haven't I?" Moa sounded pleased.

"Absolutely," I agreed. "So will you take the baby
to Queen Patchouli if I can't?"

"Yes," Moa said, straightening slightly. "On my
honor."

Exhausted after a long, hard day, we both suc-
cumbed to the rocking motion of the harnesses and
fell asleep. The larger birds had powerful wings and
flew all night. The smaller ones hitched rides in Moa's
feathers and on my shoulders. Dawn was just starting
to break when Sunset sent the pigeon to wake me.
The little birds flew off and settled into escort forma-
tion beside us again.

We were flying over the outlying residential and
business districts of Castle City. In the gray light, I
could see that the cloud people's homes and shops
were so varied and unique, no two looked alike. Some
of them mimicked cauliflower mounds and ridge
spires. Several were constructed of opaque and trans-

parent bubbles connected by colorful rock-foam. My favorite had a small ice-crystal geyser on the roof. A few even looked like dart worm caves or misshapen spoongas, which made me think that at least some of the dreaded cloud people had a sense of humor—or maybe they just wanted to be left alone.

Maybe most cloud people want privacy, I thought when I realized there were no roads. Walkways—if that's what they were—meandered between some buildings. Most of those dead-ended. Many structures were built in clumps or packed tightly together in serpentine lines with no doors to the outside.

How did the mist people get around? They didn't have roads, and I hadn't seen anything that looked like cars or carts. Did they make themselves thin and fly like Moa had described? What if there was no wind?

I turned to ask Moa, but he was too far away to hear me. He was staring straight ahead.

I followed his gaze and gasped. The elegant, icicle-like spires atop the castle glistened in the light of the rising sun. Like the town around it, the castle was a huge conglomeration of rock-foam walls, bubbles, sculpted towers, and balconies. See-through tubes connected the towers and reached the gleaming white ground of the central courtyard.

A stream of fluid sped through one of the higher

tubes, like a canister in a vacuum tube at the bank. Was that how mist people traveled from one building to another? Moa had told me he missed being able to stream through tubes.

My surveillance ended abruptly when the birds swooped down into the shadows so we wouldn't be seen by curious castle eyes. Flying low over a moat filled with steam, the birds circled to the rear of the castle and ducked behind a line of cauliflower trees.

"Get ready to land!" Sunset shouted.

I watched the ground and started running before my feet touched down. I stumbled but stayed upright. Moa rolled neatly and jumped to his feet. I quickly stepped out of my harness, rolled it up, and stuffed it into my pack. Then I untangled Moa's carry ropes and put that string away, too. I might need it again.

Most of the flock immediately took off for the safety of the wilds, but Sunset lingered to thank me again. "All the birds in Aventurine will know of your great deed and sing songs in your name, Trinity." He touched my face with his feathered wing. "Farewell, friend."

I wiped away a tear as the red and black bird flew away.

"Why are you leaking?" Moa asked with concern.

"It's not a problem, Moa," I said. "Humans leak a little when we're sad and sometimes when we're happy, too."

"Oh." Moa didn't look convinced. "When old mist people start to leak, they drip, drip, drip until they're all gone."

I hadn't given any thought to the life cycle of cloud people or if they died of old age, but it brought a vital question to mind. "How are you born?"

"When two people want a child, they go to a special pool of life," Moa explained. "If all conditions are right, a third little mist person is created by the pool."

"Oh." I checked my compass, hoping Moa didn't ask about my life cycle. I did not want to explain!

The baby's light was much brighter and blinking much faster. We were almost on top of the location. "Is there a pool near here?"

"Yes, the Morning Dew collection pool," Moa said, pointing. The direction matched the location of the baby's light on my compass.

"That's where the baby will be born," I said as I started walking. "Let's go."

We ran across a narrow strip of cleared land and took cover in a maze of foam-rock formations and spongy pink bushes with silver-blue blossoms. Moa led the way through the labyrinth, moving quickly but staying low so we wouldn't be seen. He stopped suddenly, at the exact moment I heard excited voices nearby.

I checked to make sure we were downwind, remembering that Moa said cloud people were sensitive to smells, and then carefully parted the branches of a bush to peek out and got my first glimpse of cloud people the king hadn't changed. Ten or twelve were gathered around a crystal pool. They seemed to be guarding it.

They were human in form with two legs, two arms, a torso, and one head. And like humans and fairies, no two mist people were identical. Among the group, some were tall and spindly and some were short and round with several variations in between. They seemed to prefer apple, pear, and orange torso shapes, but they could change their looks at will.

As I watched, one person's foamy white hair zipped back into his or her head like a kid slurping in spaghetti. The white hair was replaced with a lavender cap that matched a lavender vest and trousers. Some carried four-foot poles that might have been weapons or measures of an individual's status. The only physical features they had in common were large round eyes like pools of black ink and mouths that looked like the suckers on squid tentacles. As Moa made a point of telling me earlier, mist people did not have noses and couldn't smell.

But they could talk, and I heard every word.

"The sun has risen," a slim person said. The voice was melodious and sounded female. She was wearing a flowing red robe. "Are we sure this mystical child will be born here today, Voog?"

"Yes, yes!" a very thin mist man said in a quavering voice. With sunken eyes and two black patches on his arms, I assumed Voog was old and leaking.

The man in lavender glared at the old man. "Omens can be wrong."

"Not today," the old man said. Voog must have been some kind of prophet or a seer.

"Old scholars can be wrong, too!" a chubby man scoffed.

"Not today!" Voog snapped, and smacked the end of his pole on the ground. Blue lightning shot out of the other end.

It's a weapon! I wasn't sure what an electrical charge would do to a mist person, but I knew it would hurt Moa and me.

"I hope Voog is right!" A younger man stepped forward. "The child isn't ours, but it belongs to someone."

"The fairies wouldn't dare," the woman in red said.

"More likely it's from one of the solid clans on the tree," the young man surmised. "Perhaps it will give them an excuse to invade."

"Anything found in the queen's garden belongs to her and the king," Voog said. "They might keep it, or they might ask a ransom."

"What would he want?" Swirling lines appeared in the lavender man's face, as though he was puzzled.

"I'd ask for the tree." The young man's mouth puckered, like a smile. "Then no outsiders could *ever* come to the Cantigo Uplands again."

"If the child lives." The old man's words rendered everyone silent.

What does he mean? I thought back over everything Queen Patchouli had said about the birth.

"She must be held by a fairy-godmother-in-training in order to materialize —"

"Anyone who is not truly of mist cannot survive long here," the old man said.

I was so intent on the conversation I didn't hear Moa crawl over to me.

"What's going on?" he whispered.

"They know a baby is about to be born," I said, "but they don't know who or what she is."

"That's good," the bird said.

"Yes, but that's not all." I looked him in the eye, my expression grave and troubled. "Since she's not of the mist, the baby will die if I don't hold her."

Moa looked stricken. "But they'll catch you!"

"Yes," I agreed, "but I *have* to show myself to save the new fairy queen."

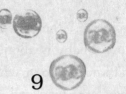

9

Born of Mist

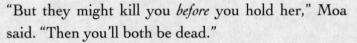

"But they might kill you *before* you hold her," Moa said. "Then you'll both be dead."

He was right, but I stood firm. It was a matter of honor and duty. My mother and grandmother would not have sacrificed a baby to save themselves.

And I would not betray Queen Patchouli's trust.

"The water is churning," the red lady whispered.

Voog nodded. "Then it won't be long now."

I put my arms around Moa's neck and hugged him. I hadn't wanted him on my journey, but he had proven himself to be invaluable. And more than that, he was a true friend.

The big bird rested his beak on my shoulder. "They'll insult me, but they won't hurt me. I could shield you."

"No." I stepped back and smiled. "As soon as the baby is solid, I'll get her away somehow. You have to hide and stay free in case I need help."

"I won't let you down," Moa said.

"I know." With nothing more to say, I walked to an opening in the shrubs to wait. The cloud people were as anxious and curious about the imminent birth as I was.

"How long will its liquid cohesion last after we take it out of the pool?" the young cloud man asked.

"A few minutes," Voog said, "perhaps a little longer. It doesn't matter. According to the omens, we don't have the one thing it needs to survive."

I perked up. Did the old man know that a fairy-godmother-in-training was the one thing? If so, my chances of staying alive had just improved a lot. But since King Shyne wanted the baby to trade or ransom, escaping with the new fairy queen would be more difficult.

"I brought a burial bowl just in case." The lavender man held up a crystal container.

"The king can't trade a bowl of water for anything valuable," the chubby man complained.

"It's forming!" the red woman announced.

The old man slid into the water, and the other cloud people closed in around the crystal pool. With their backs turned and their attention on the baby, they didn't notice me walk out of the maze. I paused a few feet back.

I had a clear view of Voog. His upper body slowly sank. The motion was so fluid I assumed he flattened his legs like the spoonga had flattened to catch the sled. A moment later, Voog returned to his original height holding a wet lump of mist baby.

I almost gasped. She looked like a potato with stumps where her head, arms, and legs should be.

"It looks normal," the woman in red said.

"Perfect for now," Voog agreed as he came out of the pool.

"Oh, good!" I spoke aloud, and clamped my hand to my mouth as all heads turned to look.

Three of the mist men raised their lightning poles and started toward me.

"No!" Voog shouted.

The guards stopped moving, but they did not lower their weapons or take their black eyes off me.

"Who are you?" the red woman asked.

"Trinity Jones of the Ananya Lineage," I said.

"A fairy-godmother-in-training?" Voog asked.

The others exchanged horrified glances.

"Fairies are not welcome in the Cantigo

Uplands," the cranky chubby guy said. "This intrusion will cost you your life."

"If you kill me, it will cost that *baby's* life." My voice was steady but my knees were shaking. "I have to hold her."

"How do you know it's a girl?" Voog held my gaze with a challenging stare.

I did not want to give away the child's identity or destiny. I bluffed. "So the omens say, do they not?"

"So they do." The old man's black eyes softened when he looked down at the newborn mist.

Voog's concern for an infant intruder's welfare was a surprise. Something had caused the baby to arrive among the hostile cloud people rather than among a doting fairy clan. Was the location connected to the big change Queen Patchouli expected? Was the new queen, a fairy born of mist, the catalyst that would help fairies and cloud people become friends?

Voog held out the baby. "Come and take her. She's beginning to seep."

The others objected but did not try to stop me when I stepped forward. Voog pressed the slippery little mist into my arms. I held my breath, afraid that the new Queen of Aventurine would dribble to death through my trembling hands. But when the translucent bundle of water began to change, my panic became awed wonder.

The stumps expanded into plump baby arms and legs with tiny fingers and toes. Two ears, two eyes, a nose, and a mouth blossomed on her heart-shaped face. It took less than a minute for the soggy lump to become a baby fairy. With a mop of black curls and a pair of dainty blue wings, she was the most precious thing I had ever seen.

And when she opened her big blue eyes, *I* was the first thing she saw. She wiggled and yawned and then scrunched up her beautiful face and started to cry.

"Is it dying?" the young mist man asked.

"She's just cold." I pulled the silky bark sling-sled out of my pack, wrapped it around the baby, and then held her close. "It's all right, baby," I cooed.

She stopped crying and snuggled against me. I wished I could call her by name, but she wouldn't have one until we got back to the Willowood for her naming ceremony.

The cloud people had other plans.

I was so enchanted by the darling little fairy that I wasn't prepared when the mist guards surrounded me. They aimed their lightning poles, and I had no doubt they would strike if provoked. When Voog took the baby back, I didn't resist. I couldn't risk having a stray electrical discharge hit her.

"Where are you taking her?" I asked as the old man and his entourage walked away.

"To the king!" the lavender man shouted.

I looked toward the maze and caught a glimpse of Moa peeking out of the bushes. I kept my eye on the bird and yelled, hoping he'd get the message. "I'm going with the baby!"

Moa poked his head out and nodded.

When the guards prodded me with their poles, I moved. The baby had been changed into a fairy, but she still needed to be rescued. I had to stay close, which meant I had to jog to keep up. Mist people moved very fast and seemed to float across the ground. I just couldn't tell how.

The Trinity-needs-to-know compulsion kicked in. "Can I see the bottom of your feet?" I asked a guard.

"No," he said. "Keep moving."

Another guard, worried that something was wrong, looked at the underside of his large, flattened foot. Hundreds of cilia wiggled on the bottom. When all the wormlike legs moved at once, it must create a gliding effect.

The procession took the long way around the maze, but I caught flashes of Moa as he followed. When we reached an open strip of land, the bird hung back so he wouldn't be seen.

After crossing the line of cauliflower trees, the mist people turned onto a wide foam-paved path that circled the castle. A variety of pastel-colored ferns, flowers, and shrubs grew in gardens along the way, and the mist people picked leaves as they passed. They removed the liquid with their puckered mouths and then dropped the dry remains. The path absorbed the dead leaves.

The grounds had been deserted when the birds flew me over the castle at dawn. Now there were several people out for a morning stroll. They all shrank back when I walked by, as though a solid person would contaminate them. Being shunned hurt, but I ignored them and watched a group of mist kids in an open field. They were playing a game that reminded me of slinky leapfrog. They transformed into streams of water and arced over each other, twisting and turning and going higher and higher until one stream bounced off another and lost.

I added another bit of information to my Cloud People Fact File: Whatever held mist people together prevented them from mixing.

When we turned onto the path leading up to the castle, everyone fell into single file behind Voog. Since we had flown in from the other side, this was my first glimpse of the huge, half-arc bridge that spanned the steaming moat. The bridge incline started well away from the banks of the waterway and curved high overhead to connect with the castle wall.

I suddenly realized why the bridge was so high and the path around the castle was so far away. The mist people wanted to keep a safe margin between them and the moat. Boiling water would scald me, but I bet it would really hurt, maybe even instantly kill, cloud people.

"Why doesn't the hot water melt the moat walls?" I asked, letting curiosity override caution.

This time the guard answered. "The moat is made of rocks brought from the outsider lands below a very long time ago."

"What keeps the water hot?" I asked.

"Dragon lilies," the guard said. "They multiply, grow, and decompose so fast they give off a tremendous amount of heat."

"They only grow naturally in one valley in the far reaches of Aventurine," another guard added.

The guards tensed when I moved closer to the bridge wall for a closer look. Looking down through the rising steam, I could just make out the red leaves that shot to the surface of the boiling water and then suddenly shriveled and died. Despite my prisoner status, I was amazed and impressed.

Like rulers everywhere, the king and queen of the Cantigo Uplands needed protection and security. In a world of water-based beings, the burning dragon lily technology was totally effective.

The bridge ended at a tall, narrow opening in the outside wall. Mist people compressed slightly to walk through the entrance. It was barely wide enough for me, so I turned sideways to fit. In contrast, the interior of the castle was immense, and I immediately went into gawk mode again.

Small clouds floated around a huge central courtyard under a crystalline dome. Some of the clouds drifted. Others seemed to be powered by something. I couldn't quite figure out what. They acted like chariots, carrying riders to and fro. One swooped down closer, and I saw that bubble creatures were acting like horses, pulling the small clouds around. Other mist people glided along walkways, rode lifts up and down, or became streams of water that traveled through the elaborate system of tubes. The air was filled with perfumes. Lucky for me, since that would make it harder for them to detect me if I needed to sneak around later.

Most of the mist people dressed in pastels, and the rainbow hues were also reflected in crystal basins and sculptures. I wanted to ask if the lady wearing red was an exception to the pastel rule. Did bright colors represent higher status, or did they reveal the people who weren't concerned with fitting in?

The question dropped to the bottom of my priority list when the guards steered me into an alcove. Voog continued on with the baby. I had to convince him to keep me close.

"You don't know what to feed her!" I shouted. I didn't know what baby fairies ate, either, but I had a better idea than people who sucked juice out of plants.

"Quiet!" a guard ordered.

I shut up and watched Voog take the baby into another alcove with the red lady and the young man.

I staggered as the floor began to move down. The elevator was wide open on the front, but I was too busy watching Voog's lift descend to be frightened when we picked up speed. I lost sight of the old man and the baby when they got off on the ground floor and entered a large oval doorway.

That must be the throne room or cloud room or whatever they call King Shyne's seat of power, I thought.

It would not be hard to find once I was free.

My lift continued down past the courtyard floor into a dark gray mist that cloaked the lower levels. The elevator didn't lurch to a stop but settled gently into the cushioning cloud floor. I stepped off without being asked rather than wait for the guards to prod or shock me.

"Go that way!" A guard pointed to the left.

I had a very bad feeling as I walked down a dark

corridor. The walls were solid with no doors or windows. We passed two open doorways. The cells were the size of closets, and the walls were a foot thick.

When the mist men shoved me into the next open cell, my suspicions about dungeon security were confirmed. A guard touched the outside wall, and that was the last thing I saw before the doorway sealed shut with foam-rock.

I was trapped in total darkness with no way out.

10

The Great Cloud Getaway

I tried not to panic.

On the bright side, the guards had not taken my things, and the feather was still in my pack. Since the mist men had never seen a fairy-godmother-in-training, they may have thought the equipment was part of me. The kite resembled wings and the baby had imprinted with wings.

"Lucky for me," I mumbled as I retrieved the feather.

With no light, I explored the door and walls with my fingers. The surface was smooth with no imperfections. Did Queen Patchouli know how the cloud dungeon worked when she gave me the feather? The lock was on the outside of the cell. I couldn't reach it with the quill. Then, remembering that I had planned to use the feather as a weapon against Kasandria

before I discovered it was a
magical key —

My mind reeled, and I
froze.

A lot of odd things had
happened since I woke up
in Aventurine, and somewhere
along the line I had begun to accept
them without trying to explain every
little thing. But when had I concluded that magic
was real? My mother had always insisted it was part
of my heritage, and for thirteen years I had rejected
the idea as impossible.

I liked order and rules so I knew what to expect.

I never knew what to expect in the fairy world.
There was a surprise, a challenge, or something unbe-
lievably incredible around every corner, or rather up
every tree branch and on every cloud.

And I had loved every magical minute.

Except for the melon mush, Hoon, and Kasandria.

And being locked in a dungeon.

I ran my finger along the edge of the soft feather.
Magic was the only rational explanation for the quill's
ability to unlock any lock.

And the dark cell would be no exception.

"Do your stuff, feather," I said as I placed the
pointed quill against the rock.

Nothing happened. But I refused to give up. I began methodically moving the quill back and forth along the walls. The feather was quiet in my hand until it hit the back corner. The foam-rock on the rear wall was much thinner, and the quill sliced through it.

"Yes!" I hissed softly, and paused.

Why had the mist men eliminated doors and windows to prevent escapes and then built a back wall that a determined prisoner could punch through?

There had to be something on the other side that was more terrifying than being in the king's jail.

I cut a small opening to look through, but I just uncovered more cloud material. It wasn't as dense as foam-rock, and after enlarging the hole, I made a space behind the wall by pulling gobs of it into the cell. The spongy cloud stuff ran about two feet out from the rear of the cell and along the outside of the underground wall. When I tried to make the space deeper, I hit hard rock that the quill couldn't even scratch.

Real rocks from below that enclosed the boiling moat, I realized. The rocks weren't warm to the touch, but they were more secure than solid foam-rock walls for keeping mist people confined.

I couldn't leave the cell until I made some adjustments. I took the kite off my harness, removed the string and the silky bark covering from the frame, loosened the middle cross tie, and then rolled it all up.

If necessary, I could put the kite back together in a hurry. For now, it was compact enough to fit through tight spaces. I slipped the rolled kite lengthwise under the harness straps on my back.

Holding the feather in my teeth, I tunneled with my hands, moving the spongy cloud behind me as I worked my way toward the cell next to mine. When I placed the quill against the rear wall, it easily cut through the thin foam-rock. I was inside the cell in less than a minute, and the doorway was still open.

I could only see a few feet through the dark gray mist outside the doorway. Although I was pretty sure the corridor wasn't patrolled, I paused to listen. There was no sound—no cries for help or squeaky mist rats or slushy footsteps. I put the feather in my pack and retraced my way back to the lift.

The elevator wasn't there, and I turned left toward the interior of the castle before someone could ride a lift down and find me. I moved cautiously, keeping my hand on the wall. Ten minutes later, I reached a transport tube going up.

The twelve-inch tube was constructed of transparent, superdense cloud material and was attached to a not-so-dense track. After a little experimentation, I realized I could grip the outside of the tube with my arms and make toeholds by jamming my feet into the track.

No different from climbing a rock wall back home, I thought as I started up.

Nothing extraordinary happened on the lower levels, but just before I reached the ground floor, I hit a junction. While I straddled the midpoint of the intersecting tubes, two mist people streams rushed toward me from opposite directions. I froze, terrified. What if they could see me? I watched in fascination, expecting them to stop or sound an alarm.

The mist-people-don't-mix rule was absolute. Both streams elongated into thin ribbons, and the travelers passed each other unharmed. I hoped they had been going too fast to notice the fairylike invader clinging to the outside of their public transportation system.

The tube entered the main castle behind a line of parked clouds. I used my feather knife to cut a larger opening in the floor and peeked out. The large court-yard was bustling with activity.

Official-looking mist people in pastel robes con-ferred in groups or hurried in and out of doorways as though their business was of extreme importance. People in simpler outfits stood by bins filled with leaves and flowers, which they gave to anyone who stopped. Other mist people fed leaves to resting bub-ble beasts.

Filling up to power the cloud carriages, I thought with a smile.

My position was directly across from the oval doorway where Voog had gone with the fairy baby, but the courtyard was too crowded and dangerous to cross.

I ducked down when a mom and two mist children boarded a parked cloud nearby.

"We want to go outside," one child said.

"Outside!" the smaller one repeated.

"Nobody flies a cloud outside," the mom replied. She pushed a bubble creature into a hollow tube on one end of the cloud. "If a strong wind comes along, we'd be swept away and lost in the lands below. Never to be seen again," she added in an ominous tone.

The kids' black eyes widened and shivers rippled across their watery backs. They huddled in the middle of the cloud when the mom broke a tether in two, tilted the bubble beast, and patted the creature's back. It burped, expelling bubbles, and the cloud shot upward. When the carriage reached the desired elevation, the mist mom leveled the animal and patted it again.

As the family floated away, I realized a cloud carriage would give me plenty of cover to cross the courtyard. I was pretty certain I could figure out how to drive, but the clouds parked nearby didn't have bubble creatures. I took the next best option and crept to the nearest cloud, climbed on, and broke the tether.

Mist people seemed to ignore drifting clouds unless the clouds hit them. Then they just pushed them aside. I wouldn't be seen, but the cloud moved so slowly it might be hours before it got to the far side of the courtyard. I had no choice but to hunker down and wait.

The floor of the cloud car hardened to hold me, but the sides remained soft and malleable. I made a rectangular hole that I could see through and still keep my head down and hidden. For the first few minutes, my cloud hovered, barely moving. Then a bubble-powered cloud bumped into it, and it shot off—straight toward the oval door.

My cloud was bumped and sent sailing off in several directions before it finally came close to the throne room wall.

Two stories up.

I made another hole in the side of the cloud for my arm and held on to a tube track. Looking down, I saw that the oval opening was much larger than it appeared from the far side of the castle. Two guards with lightning poles flanked the door. Then suddenly, four more armed men rushed out. All six altered shape to appear more rigid and battle ready.

It seemed like they had just gone on alert.

Did they know I had escaped?

If so, they probably didn't know where to look.

Escaped prisoners usually leave the building.

A large blue cloud car pulled alongside me, carrying a regal mist person who had to be Queen Sonja. Slightly larger than other mist people, she wore sunshine-yellow puffs on her head and sky-blue robes. Two mist ladies in the car with her controlled bubble beasts.

I exhaled slowly. The guards weren't looking for me. They were awaiting the arrival of the queen.

"It's a fairy baby, Your Majesty," one of the ladies said. "She's not your responsibility."

"It's still a baby," Queen Sonja pointed out. "And it's probably hungry."

"What do fairies eat?" the other lady asked.

"I heard they dine on bugs and plant roots they pull out of dirt." The first lady made a disgusted noise. "And they grind it all up with the hard claws in their mouths."

"Disgusting," the queen said.

Time to catch a ride, I thought as I slipped my arm through the side of my car. I grabbed the tether dangling from the queen's car as it passed and held on when my cloud was jerked forward.

I wasn't sure what my next move would be. A lot depended on whether anyone asked Queen Sonja why she had a second cloud in tow. But at least I was getting closer to the baby every second.

I'd worry about how to get away after I had the little fairy in my arms.

I worried about Moa now. Where was he? Could he get off the cloud domain without falling? There had to be plenty of nice people in Aventurine who would welcome a bird with such a good heart, even if he couldn't fly. Like the Curipoo!

Thinking about Jango and Targa gave me a boost. I *had* to get back to the Willowood with Queen Patchouli's successor. I had promised my friends.

Through the peephole, I saw the six guards form a line between the throne room door and the courtyard. As the queen's car descended and turned to enter, I held my breath, but no one broke rank to separate the two clouds as we passed through the doorway.

King Shyne and Queen Sonja's throne room was plain compared to how I had always imagined a throne room would look. Rather than being decorated with gold, silver, and jewels, it was pastel blue with a blazing yellow sunburst on the wall behind the massive, fluffy cloud thrones. Sunlight streamed in through a huge lattice-covered window higher on the same wall. Cultivated garden patches with leaves and flowers were randomly placed around the cavernous room. Four catlike mist animals romped in a corner. A few mist people lounged on clouds, snacked on leaves, or waited on the sidelines to speak with the king, a privilege that was difficult if not impossible today.

The fairy baby was lying in a cloud cradle at the king's feet, and she was screaming.

I waited and watched, hatching a plan.

"Can you make it stop?" King Shyne pleaded with the queen when she stepped out of her car.

"I've tried everything I can think of," Voog said. He sounded distraught.

"I'm sure you have, Voog." Queen Sonja gently touched the baby's wet face. "You can go. We appreciate everything you've done."

Voog bowed slightly and backed away. As he left, the two ladies-in-waiting left the queen's cloud car and walked to a garden at the far end of the chamber. None of the other mist people were anxious to get near the fairy child, either, which simplified things for me.

"Did you feed her?" the queen asked her husband.

"We tried," the king said. "I had infant formula brought in, but she doesn't like leaf sprouts."

The king appeared to be more distressed than the old man, and the queen left the baby to console him.

There was no more time to think. I jumped out of my cloud car, picked up the baby, and got into the queen's car. The hungry little fairy continued to cry after I placed her on the floor, but feeding her had to wait until we were safely away. Remembering everything I had seen, I tilted both bubble beasts and patted their backs.

"Intruder!" someone shouted.

"Where?" the king asked, looking frantic.

By the time the royal couple discovered the baby was gone, I was fifteen feet in the air and climbing. Then I re-aimed the bubble beasts and headed straight for the lattice. As we neared, I draped the bark sling over the baby's face.

The delicate crisscrossed network of ice crystals and cloud was as fragile as it looked. The queen's carriage plowed through it, sending a rain of shattered ice falling on the throne room below.

"Get her back!" the king shouted.

"But don't hurt the baby!" the queen commanded.

"Yee-haw!" I yelled as the car sailed out of the castle, over the steaming moat, and into the clear blue skies above the cloud domain.

Luckily, the winds were light, and the cloud wasn't in danger of being carried away. I had to feed the baby, but I needed both hands on the bubble creatures to direct them. I hoped Moa had done as I asked: hide and stay free in case I needed help.

I steered low over the maze and found the big

bird sitting between two shrubs near the crystal pool of life. He looked frightened when he spotted my carriage and jumped up to run.

"Moa!" I shouted. "It's me!"

The bird stopped and looked back up. "Trinity! You came back to get me!"

"And you waited for me!" I laughed. Then I realized that I wasn't quite sure how to land. Hoping my logic was correct, I aimed the bubble beasts up and tapped their backs. The cloud descended, but it went down too fast. At the last second, I reversed the beasts and tapped again.

The cloud carriage hovered without touching the ground.

"Where did you learn to drive?" Moa asked as he hopped in.

"I took the castle crash course," I joked. "Which way to the edge near the tree?"

The bird pointed with his head.

As we sped back into the sky, the king's air force zoomed out of the castle. We had a head start, but the mist men's cloud carriages were equipped with fully fueled, rested bubble beasts. They would catch up eventually—unless we got to the border first.

"Can you steer?" I asked Moa. "I'll take care of the little fairy queen."

"Yes," the bird said as we switched places.

I picked up the little warm bundle and carefully brushed away any lingering bits of ice and cloud left over from crashing through the lattice. Moving aside the sling's fabric, I revealed the baby's squalling face. So far, Queen Patchouli's assurance that I'd have everything I needed to complete the mission had been 100 percent true. I doubted she had overlooked the fact that babies have to eat. With the new queen cradled in my arms, I put the never-gone sweet potato up to her tiny mouth. The potato end elongated like a baby bottle, and the little fairy began to drink. After a few minutes, she was sound asleep.

I put her down and picked up the kite.

"Now we can hear ourselves think," I said as I fastened the cross sticks together.

"And talk," Moa said. "You can't fly a cloud carriage off the Cantigo Uplands. The bubble beasts won't survive."

"I wouldn't do anything to hurt them," I said. "The carriage just has to get us to the edge. The kite flew us up here, and it will get us down." A sudden realization hit me. "Except—"

"You can only take one of us with you," the bird

said matter-of-factly. "And you have to take the baby. That's your mission."

"Yes." I felt awful about leaving Moa behind. "Will you be okay?"

"Are you kidding?" The bird puffed up again. "I was turned into a bird with no wings, almost killed by a mean fairy, barely escaped being eaten by a spoonga, and carried high over land by birds. Of course I'll be okay."

I took the feather out of my pack and tucked it into the feathers on his back.

"I want you to have this," I said. "So you'll never forget that you're a hero."

"I'll keep it on one condition," Moa said.

"What's that?" I picked up the silky bark kite covering.

"The kite didn't fly us up here, Trinity. *You* did."

"No, the kite—"

The bird cut me off. "The kite is a crutch. You're a fairy-godmother-in-training. You have magic. You have to trust it."

"What are you saying?" I asked.

"I'm saying you don't need a kite." Moa looked me in the eye. "You can fly. You just have to believe it."

I frowned, wanting to believe but not trusting it. I stopped talking and concentrated on the kite. When it was complete, I set it aside and started working on a belly sling for the baby. I finished that just as the cloud carriage cleared the first of the three ridges Moa and I had climbed yesterday.

"How close are the mist men?" Moa asked.

"They're gaining," I said, "but I think we'll beat them."

"You'll make it," the bird said.

Maybe not, I thought when the cloud car almost stalled over the second ridge.

"What's happening?" I asked.

"We're running out of gas," Moa said. "You better get the little fairy queen ready to travel."

While the bird coaxed the exhausted bubble beasts to keep going, I eventually managed to get the harness on backward and fasten it. Then I put the wrapped baby into the sling across my chest and tied her to me with unbreakable string. I stuffed the potato into the pack beside her and picked up the kite, and we were ready to go.

My timing couldn't have been better. Moa landed the cloud car at the bottom of the hill where we had first seen the spoonga trail. The edge was close. I just had to run without falling into a crater or hitting a geyser.

"Go," Moa said as the king's cloud cars cleared the top of the hill. "I'll hold them off."

I hesitated. "I can't just leave you! You could die."

"You don't have a choice. I'm saving you now,

just like you saved me. My debt is paid." Moa shoved me with his beak.

I knew the life debt wasn't the only reason for his stand. Moa was sacrificing himself because he cared about me and the baby queen and the future of Aventurine and the cloud people who had treated him so badly.

"The mist men won't fly off the edge," Moa went on. "The bubble beasts will shut down, and the guards don't want to fall. Now get out of here!"

I threw my arms around Moa for a quick good-bye hug and then ran.

I ran so fast I didn't see the hooked outcropping of rock on one of the formations. I ducked at the last minute, but I didn't duck down far enough. The rock snagged my kite and ripped it in half.

Behind me, I heard the mist men shouting at Moa. "Get out of the way, solid!"

"What?" Moa shouted back. "Are you talking to me?"

I skidded to a stop two feet from the end of the Cantigo Uplands.

I only had half a kite left. It was useless. I dropped it, put my arms around the baby, and looked down at the top of the tree.

Was Moa right? Could I have flown up to the cloud domain without the kite?

I stepped to the very edge, thinking about Moa's words: *"You have magic. You can fly. You just have to believe it."*

"There she is!" a man's voice yelled.

With the future Queen of Aventurine tied to my chest, I spread my arms and swan dived off the cloud.

11

Wings

I spread my arms and legs to catch the wind and fell, not fast like a ton of rocks, but steadily, past the top of the tree in ten seconds. My stomach was in my throat and strands of my hair stuck in my teeth.

The baby laughed, and the sound snapped me to my senses: I had to fly or we would both die.

I closed my eyes, drew my legs together, dipped my right arm, and visualized a slow, graceful arc. Something tingled inside me, and I felt a warmth seep out from my gut to my fingers and toes. When I swooped into a wobbly but controlled turn, my eyes popped open.

I was flying!

No kite, no wings, just me.

On-my-own flying!

As I completed the curve, I angled my body

up and soared higher. I banked again, completed another long lazy turn, and then flew in a wide circle around the treetop. After a few more practice turns, every movement came naturally, just as they did in my dreams.

"I did it!" I laughed, and glanced at the Cantigo Uplands overhead. I wanted to fly back, to show Moa he was right, but I couldn't take the chance. The new Queen of Aventurine was safe now, and I had to take her back to the Willowood.

But there were no rules that said I couldn't have fun doing it.

"Okay, baby!" I shouted. "Let's see what we can do!"

The little fairy giggled as I headed downward in a slow spiraling course.

Everything on Kasandria's old branch looked so different I almost missed it. The dead vines and rotting brush that had mirrored the fallen fairy's black heart were still visible here and there, but new leaves, vines, and bunches of flowers were taking over. Dozens of birds perched on secondary branches, and their songs filled the air.

The white chicken spotted me from a nest it had built in an old feeding dish. "The lock lady's back!"

The birds were still weak from their ordeal as Kasandria's captives and didn't fly out to greet me. Instead, they flapped their wings and called out their thanks and good wishes. I dipped to the left and then to the right to acknowledge them before continuing on to the hot springs.

"When you're older, go to that branch for a hot bath," I told the little queen. "It's very relaxing."

I flew a long way out from the tree to avoid Hoon's territory and gave the infant queen strict instructions.

"Stay away from Hoon and his awful little toad-men," I said sternly. "He calls himself the Keeper of the Cloud Pine Forest, but I think he just made it up. He is *not* a nice guy."

The baby couldn't understand me, but my tour guide patter helped cement the memories in my mind. I didn't want to forget a single detail of the journey, especially the friendly Curipoo.

I saw the kites flying off the Curipoo branch from a distance. In the short time I had been gone, Jango and Targa had made a dozen kites and taught others to fly them.

I couldn't take the time to land, but I wanted to let them know I had survived my mission.

I buzzed the branch.

"Hey!" Jango yelled.

"That's Trinity!" Targa shouted, and waved. "Trinity!"

"I made it!" I shouted as I flew by again. "Your kites are wonderful!"

"Everybody wants one!" Jango yelled. "Come see!"

I wanted to stop, but I knew the Curipoo would keep me too long. I just waved and flew out of sight around the massive trunk.

I suddenly realized I didn't know how to get back to the Willowood. Even if I knew how, I couldn't return through the magic mirror portal. The baby couldn't be expected to keep her eyes closed during the ride. It was just too dangerous.

I landed on the end of a branch and scanned the sparse secondary branches. I could take off quickly if something dangerous threatened, but all I saw were small brown lizards and blue bugs. Satisfied we were safe, I pulled out my pendant and opened it.

"Oooh," the baby cooed.

"The inside is even better." I pressed the clasp and held the open disk for the baby to see. Then I asked for directions. "Show me the way back home."

The gizmos whirred and the filaments glowed. A blue mist swirled and slowly cleared to reveal a compass with an arrow pointing toward a waterfall—the first landmark on the way back to the Willowood. With the open pendant in my hand and the baby snug against my chest, I flew off the branch.

I intended to stay above the fog that shrouded the dense forest, but the gray mist enveloped everything within its realm. No matter how high I rose, the fog closed in around me. Visibility was near zero, but the lighted compass buzzed whenever I veered off course and kept buzzing until I was headed in the right direction again.

Now I knew how my mom felt when she had to fly a jetliner through heavy rain: It wasn't fun, and having to rely on instruments took skill and concentration.

Before long, I could see the vague outline of mountain peaks. As I drew nearer, the fog dissipated to give me a clear view of a waterfall. The river plunged through a break in a cliff into a deep pool. I checked the compass, expecting to see the next landmark, but the arrow still pointed to the waterfall.

Is that a hint to stop and rest? I was tired from the physical exertion and the tension of flying blind, and the baby was hungry. She was starting to fuss. Still, although I wanted to land, I didn't know if I could get airborne again from the ground.

I circled to make sure it was safe to land. The riverbank was wide and grassy at the top of the cliff, and a rocky ledge jutted out over the waterfall, providing a nice launch platform.

I banked to slow my speed. I decided to land feet-first, like flying superheroes did in movies. If something went wrong, I might break an ankle, but I wouldn't smash my face or the baby into the ground. At ten feet, I brought my legs down—and hovered!

"Cool!" I exclaimed as I lowered myself to the ground.

The little queen clearly disagreed; she started to cry.

I sat down on a moss-covered rock and pulled the fairy food out of the pack. I was hungry, too, but I only took a quick bite. The sweet potato replenished the part I had bitten off and then adjusted to fit the baby's mouth. Her cries became sobs that quieted as she filled her tummy.

Cradling the baby helped me relax, and the aches in my arms and legs seemed to magically ease. In fact, as I glanced about, I realized that everything in the small glen was responding to the new queen's presence.

Bell flowers jingled, and woodpeckers drummed a lively beat on the trees. The grass grew taller and greener, and flowers blossomed in bouquets of violet, pink, yellow, white, and blue. A white rabbit hopped over and gently nuzzled the baby's cheek.

Not quite a proper hongi, I thought. In the traditional Maori greeting, people touched foreheads and noses to trade the breath of life. The hongi signified that one was not a visitor but belonged to the land. I was sure the rabbit meant the same thing.

The baby would be the queen of everyone and everything in the fairy world. She *was* Aventurine.

As soon as she finished eating, the baby fell asleep. I put the never-gone sweet potato back in the pack beside her and refreshed myself with a drink from the water pod. Then I walked out onto the rocky ledge and checked the compass.

The image had changed. Instead of one arrow, there were several tiny arrows that followed the path of the river below right through the Willowood.

"It's the creek!" I exclaimed. The sound of rushing water had helped me get oriented when I first woke up in the fairy world. Now it was a reassuring sign that I had almost completed my mission. I checked the sling to make sure the baby was safely tucked in. Reminding myself that the journey wasn't over yet, I took a deep breath and imagined myself leaping into the air. Warmth flooded through me, and I shot up into the sky.

I flew above the trees as I followed the winding course of the river. Although the lower route might have been more interesting, my first priority was to deliver the baby to Queen Patchouli quickly and safely. Still, the trip wasn't totally boring.

The flora and fauna of Aventurine continued to welcome the little fairy queen.

Treetops bowed as I flew by. Rows and rows of birds in high branches chirped and whistled. When the river narrowed, a brisk wind forced me to descend, and the overhanging tree branches parted to clear a flight path. I spotted the clearing with the stone table.

"We're here!" I shouted with joy.

The creatures of the forest shouted back — roaring, squeaking, chittering, and chirping in their excitement to welcome the royal baby. Animals gathered in the willows on the edge of the glen. As I brought my feet down to land, all of the fairy queens glided out of the woods.

"It's Trinity!" Queen Honorae exclaimed.

"Of course it is," Queen Patchouli said matter-of-factly, as though no one else could possibly cause such a commotion upon arrival.

"And she brought the baby!" young Queen Blanca squealed. She was so excited she changed into a small white horse and whinnied as she romped around the field.

"Of course she did," Queen Patchouli said, as if she never had a doubt. She smiled when she stopped before me. "I am so glad to see you, Trinity, and very happy that you brought the new queen with you."

"Thank you. She's really sweet and —" The words stuck in my throat, and the rush of emotion I felt surprised me.

In a few short hours, I had grown to love the little fairy. *Like a little sister,* I thought, fighting back a tear. I didn't want to give her up, but she wasn't mine to keep.

"Can we see her?" Queen Patchouli asked gently. She seemed to understand how I felt and didn't want to rush me.

"Sure," I said as I lifted the baby out of the pack. I held her in my arms and pulled down the silky bark swaddling to show off her adorable face. "Isn't she beautiful?"

"The most beautiful baby ever," Queen Patchouli agreed.

"All new mothers think that," Mama Cocha grumped. Then she grinned and added, "But this time it's true!"

"She's so tiny!" Queen Blanca the horse exclaimed. "When can I give her pony rides?"

"Soon enough," Queen Patchouli said.

I beamed with pride as all the queens gushed over the baby. The infant fairy was, as she should be, the center of attention, but she was not the queens' only concern.

"I was so worried about you, Trinity," the blue queen said. "No one who is not of the mist has ever gone to the Cantigo Uplands and returned."

"Not that we know of and not until today, Queen Marla." Queen Mangi regarded me with relief and respect. "It must have been difficult."

"There were a few tight spots and close calls," I admitted.

"I haven't danced a step," the golden Queen Tensy said.

"But you wore a new path around the guesthouse with your constant pacing," Queen Alaina teased.

"We've done nothing but wish for your safe return." The blind Queen Carmina put a hand on my arm.

Her soothing touch removed the last traces of stress as I looked into the faces of the queens gathered around me. The warmth in their smiles and joy in their eyes almost made me cry. I felt guilty for doubting my mother and denying their existence for so many years.

Then suddenly, I started to collapse.

"Take her, please," I said, quickly giving the baby to Queen Patchouli.

Queen Mangi gripped my arm to steady me. "You must be exhausted!"

"You need to rest so you don't sleep through the festivities tonight," the silvery Queen Kumari said.

"I am a little tired," I said, yawning. I couldn't keep my eyes open.

I stretched and inhaled the scent of a fresh flower bouquet. My mom usually chose spice and herbal-scented air fragrances. This new one smelled just like Aventurine.

Then I opened my eyes. I wasn't in my New York City bedroom. I was lying on a soft pad in a fairy cottage. The scent of flowers did not come from a spray bottle but from climbing morning glories and rosebushes growing on the walls.

I had been so tired when I arrived I hadn't noticed anything except the comfy bed of feathers of moss.

How long was I asleep? I yawned and stretched again. The light shining through the round windows had the golden cast of late afternoon fading to dusk, the same as when I dozed off. *Has a whole night and day passed?*

That wouldn't surprise me. The instant Queen Patchouli took the baby, my legs had given out.

The worried fairy queens had offered me food and water, but I was too exhausted to eat. Even so, Queen Patchouli made me swallow a small, spiced honey ball before she let me lie down.

I sat up, ran my fingers through my tangled hair, and scratched my itchy nose. I was still wearing my tunic and leggings, but my shoes and harness were neatly stacked on a stool. The Ananya necklace was around my neck.

"Rise and shine!" Queen Patchouli said as she swept in through the round, open door.

With magnificent blue wings and a glittering silver-blue gown, the Queen of Aventurine looked gorgeous. A flowered wreath with colorful streamers crowned her lustrous chestnut hair. Her smile chased away the twilight shadows in the room.

"How are you feeling?" the fairy queen asked.

"Great!" I exclaimed. "I can't believe I slept a whole day away."

"You didn't," Queen Patchouli said. "The honey ball I gave you made you rest more efficiently. You didn't want to miss the naming ceremony, did you?"

"No!" I grinned, then asked, "Is the baby okay? The cloud people had her a long time before we got away. She was really hungry, and I had to feed her sweet potato."

"The little queen is perfect!" Queen Patchouli

exclaimed. She came and laid a gentle hand on my shoulder. "Your mission was one of the most difficult I've ever assigned, and your success is an achievement of unmatched importance."

"Thanks, but I didn't do it alone," I said. "The Curipoo and the birds I rescued from Kasandria helped a lot, especially Moa."

The queen's face darkened at the mention of Kasandria's name. I suspected that evil fairies were very rare and something good fairies preferred not to think or talk about. I rattled on about my friend instead.

"Of course, Moa is really a mist person. He thinks cloud people and fairies should be friends, so King Shyne changed him into a bird. Moa sacrificed himself so the baby and I could escape." I could feel my eyes begin to water just thinking about my loyal friend.

"I see," the queen said, nodding gravely. She gave my shoulder a reassuring squeeze and released it. "Someday soon I want to hear all about your adventure and the cloud people and how the new queen was born, but right now it's time to get ready for the naming ceremony. You're the guest of honor."

"I, uh . . ." I was so overcome with emotion I didn't know what to say. "That's so . . . cool. I probably should, uh . . . clean up . . . and change," I stammered.

The climbing flowers on one wall parted to reveal

a tall wooden panel, which promptly unfolded into the wardrobe.

"I'm sure you'll find something you like in there," Queen Patchouli said.

As the queen left, three other fairies entered. They set baskets and pitchers on a table and told me they'd be nearby if I needed anything else. On her way out, the last fairy paused in a corner and pulled a vine to start a rainwater shower.

After washing with daisy-petal soap and drying off with towel moss, I felt clean as well as rested. I was also famished and eager to join the festivities. But first, I had to pick a dress that was suitable for such a momentous occasion.

Most of the gowns in the wardrobe were too frilly, flimsy, or fancy for my tastes. I only found one I liked. With a long, flowing skirt and a scooped neckline, the sky-blue dress complemented my dark hair. Diamonds were embroidered with gold thread in a band across the waist. The pattern reminded me a bit of sunbursts and Queen Sonja. If the fairy baby had been born to close the rift between cloud people and fairies, the gown was perfect for her naming ceremony.

191

As I dressed and fixed my hair, I was happy and sad. I was elated about rescuing the little queen and devastated about losing Moa. I would miss them and all the other new friends I had made in Aventurine.

Still, I smiled as I stepped outside. The new queen and I had the same birthday, and it was time to celebrate.

12

Happy Birthdays

Two fairies were waiting outside the cottage. They both wore gossamer gowns with sparkling dewdrop accents and flowered wreaths on their heads.

"Come on, Trinity!" the fairy in pink said, rising off the ground and waving for me to follow.

"Everyone is asking for you!" The second fairy hovered on wings that fluttered with excitement.

"Then let's rattle our dags!" I exclaimed, slipping into Kiwi slang.

The two fairies looked at me with perplexed expressions.

"Let's get moving!" I clarified.

They both giggled and swept off down the path.

I had to walk fast to keep up with the gliding fairies. I thought about flying with them, but I didn't have perfect control yet. One stray branch could snag and ruin my dress as quickly as the cloud rocks had destroyed my kite.

The last rays of the setting sun played off the trees as we hurried through the village of quaint houses. Not a single fairy was in sight. Even the path that followed the meandering creek through the woods was deserted.

When we reached the edge of the ceremonial clearing, I paused. The rest of the Willowood was empty because everyone was here. The queens and hundreds of fairies from all the clans had gathered for the naming of Queen Patchouli's infant successor.

"Don't dawdle!" the pink fairy teased. "Everyone wants to meet you!"

I gasped. "Me?"

"You're the fairy-godmother-in-training who survived the Cantigo Uplands and saved the future Queen of Aventurine!" the second fairy exclaimed.

I wasn't shy, but I had never been a celebrity at a major event before. I froze, stricken with stage fright.

"Queen Patchouli is waiting," the pink fairy said. "She won't start the naming ceremony without you."

Get over it, Trinity! I scolded myself, then took three deep breaths to calm my racing heart.

"Lead the way," I said with a smile.

The grassy glade was brightly lit by torches and dancing fireflies. Baskets heaped with food sat on giant toadstool tables, and lemonade flowed from crystal fountains. Garlands of ferns and flowers hung from the trees, and fairies wearing more colors than crayons gathered in kaleidoscopic clusters. Rabbits, squirrels, deer, foxes, and other forest animals wandered everywhere, accepting pats and tidbits from the fairies.

A group of fairies played music on flutes, gourd drums, and delicate stringed sticks, and a choir that included Queen Honorae sang in sweet, melodious voices. Queen Tensy and other Gold Dancers performed a graceful ballet. When the music suddenly became more energetic, Queen Mangi and the stone fairies leaped, hovered, and twirled using colored Kalis sticks as batons.

The Curipoo would love this! I thought with a smile. Their Irish jigs and do-si-dos would fit right in.

"Hi, Trinity!" Queen Blanca came abreast of me and skipped to keep pace. She wore a lacy white dress, and an entourage of small crystal ponies followed her. "If you have time later, will you tell us about the great tree?"

"I'll make time, Queen Blanca," I said.

"Goodie! I love stories." The young queen clapped her hands and ran off to join Mama Cocha and Queen Alaina by a huge basket of berries, apples, and figs.

Just beyond them, Queen Patchouli sat on a raised stone platform under an awning of braided willow branches. The baby was in her arms and a big bird that couldn't fly stood by her side.

"Moa!" I ran the rest of the way and leaped onto the platform. I threw my arms around the bird's short neck. "You're alive!"

"I'm too tough to die," the bird said, fluffing his feathers.

"What happened?" I asked, rising to my feet.

"The guards caught me," the bird said with a sigh. "Then the king officially banished me from the Cantigo Uplands and had his guards push me off the Long-Way-Down Peninsula." He paused, looking bewildered. "There's no tree under that spot."

I gasped. "How did you get here?"

"I don't know," the bird said.

I glanced at Queen Patchouli. She just rocked the baby and smiled.

I smiled back. Sometimes magic works and that's all you need to know.

"By the way, you were right," I told Moa. "I can fly!"

"I always knew you had it in you." Moa nodded his head and then motioned toward the tables loaded with food. "Can we eat now?"

"After the ceremony," I said.

Queen Patchouli motioned for Moa and me to stand beside her. Then she raised her hand, silencing the fairies as they gathered before her. The sea of color parted as the queens moved forward.

The blue Queen Marla guided the blind Queen Carmina, who seemed to glow. Queen Blanca stood in front of Mama Cocha, jiggling with impatience until the older queen placed gentle, calming hands on her shoulders. Queens Mangi, Honorae, and Tensy made an unlikely trio in delicate yellow, black leather, and gold. Queen Kumari gleamed in silver, and Queen Alaina's kimono shimmered with all the creatures of the worlds.

My mother had only met Queen Patchouli. I couldn't wait to tell her about all the rest.

A hush fell over the glade. Even the crickets were quiet as Queen Patchouli moved to the edge of the platform.

"A new Queen of Aventurine has been born."

Queen Patchouli's voice, as steady and strong as her reign, rang through the clearing and the surrounding woods. "Born of mist and made solid by the Ananya fairy godmother lineage, she is now of the Willowood and awaits your blessings."

One by one, the clan queens came forward to welcome the baby and present their gifts.

The statuesque Queen Mangi of the warrior clan held up a small golden stick. "With this Kalis stick, the stone fairies wish you the joy of dancing and pledge to defend you, the Willowood, and all of Aventurine." Her small wings fluttered as she placed the Kalis stick in the large basket at Queen Patchouli's feet.

Queen Marla helped Queen Carmina onto the stone platform. After dropping a string of blue pearls in the basket, she stepped back to wait.

The queen with the pearly eyes placed her hand on the baby's head. "I will comfort you and soothe you if you should ever hurt, but my blessing is the hope that nothing ever does."

The baby gurgled, innocent and unaware of the great trials and responsibilities that lay ahead. I hoped such things wouldn't matter in her life for a very long time. Even fairy queens deserved to be kids, at least for a while.

Queen Kumari carried a plate with a single cupcake. She placed a tiny dollop of icing on the baby's lips. "May the sweet and beautiful things in your life abound and may the bitter be scarce."

The new queen, liking the icing and wanting more, started to cry when the silvery queen set down the cupcake and stepped aside. Queen Patchouli tried to quiet her, but the sobs didn't stop until the baby was distracted by the plants and animals living in Queen Alaina's kimono.

"May you bend like the willow in the wind and flow with the tide in a storm, never to be broken," Queen Alaina said.

Moa shifted from one foot to the other as the blessings and presentations continued. My stomach grumbled, but no one seemed to hear.

Queen Blanca and Mama Cocha came forward together.

"You will always have ponies to ride, to keep you company, and to wisely advise," the little girl said.

"And whales to teach you the ways of the sea," the older fairy added.

As Queen Blanca started to leave, she turned back and whispered, "Ponies like to play, too!"

Queen Tensy and Queen Honorae were last.

"May your step through the world always be light," the golden queen said.

"And may your voice always ring clear," Queen Honorae sang.

Then finally, when I thought *I* was going to faint from hunger, the big moment arrived.

Queen Patchouli held the baby up for all to see. "From this moment on and forever, you will be known as Asa, young Queen of the Willowood Fairies and all of Aventurine."

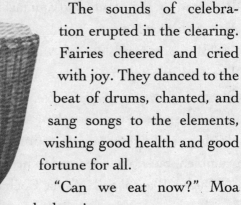

The sounds of celebration erupted in the clearing. Fairies cheered and cried with joy. They danced to the beat of drums, chanted, and sang songs to the elements, wishing good health and good fortune for all.

"Can we eat now?" Moa asked again.

"Yes, and have fun!" Queen Patchouli shooed us away. The baby, exhausted after a very long and trying naming ceremony, was asleep in her arms. She gently placed Asa in a woven willow branch cradle.

"Do they have any tasty leaves?" Moa asked.

"Let's go find out," I said.

In the interest of good manners, I filled two plates with honey cakes, dried fruit, buttered apple-nut

bread, cupcakes, berries, and flower salad—one for Moa and one for me. Moa didn't want to offend anyone by taking things out of serving bowls with his beak. Then we joined Queen Blanca and the ponies.

The young queen and I sat on toadstools, holding our plates on our laps. I put Moa's plate on a big rock, and he nibbled standing up. The ponies grazed, and in between bites, I gave them a detailed account of the beings and creatures I had met on the giant tree.

"Queen Patchouli should have invited your Curipoo friends," Queen Blanca said. "They like to have fun."

"Yes, but they don't like to leave the tree," I said.

"Was meeting Jango and Targa the best part of your mission?" Queen Blanca asked.

"No," Moa said, ruffling his feathers. "The best part was meeting me."

"Yes, absolutely," I said. "Meeting Moa *and* holding the baby queen for the first time."

After we ate, we wandered over to the fountains. I drank two glasses of lemonade and filled a glass with water for Moa. Then we joined the musical fairies. They were singing a simple song and Queen Honorae encouraged us to join in.

"You have a very pleasant voice, Trinity," the queen complimented me, but she was too polite to be honest with Moa.

I giggled. I couldn't help it. King Shyne had turned Moa into a bird that couldn't fly and that couldn't sing, either. His off-key warble was hysterical.

"Is my singing really that funny?" Moa asked, pretending to be annoyed.

"It's almost as funny as my Haka war dance," I said.

Queen Tensy heard the word *dance* and turned around. "I'd love to see it!"

I could not refuse a queen's request.

"Maori warriors danced the Haka to prepare for a fight," I explained.

I spread my feet, bent my knees, and thumped my heels repeatedly to keep a beat. I shook my fists, slapped my chest and arms, and chanted. My version of the fierce ritual didn't scare the fairies, either. Like the Curipoo, they thought it was hilarious.

When the party began to wind down, Queen Patchouli stood up to make another announcement. A tense hush fell over the crowd.

"Every now and then, someone provides an invaluable, selfless service to fairies and Aventurine that must be acknowledged and rewarded," Queen

Patchouli said. "Tonight, in gratitude for everything he did to help Trinity bring Asa home, I humbly honor Moa and grant him his fondest wish."

"Is she talking about me?" Moa asked.

"You're the only Moa I know," I said. "She's given you a wish!"

"Would you like to be a mist person again, Moa?" Queen Patchouli asked.

The bird shook his head. "No. I can't return to the Cantigo Uplands, and as a mist person, I'd be alone down here."

"There must be something you want," I said.

Moa hesitated, but only for a moment. "I want wings so I can fly," he said softly. "Then I can live with the other birds Trinity saved on the tree."

"That would be nice," I said.

"So be it." Queen Patchouli closed her eyes and raised her arms.

Feather and wind,
Wing and sky,
This noble bird can fly!

I stared, transfixed as the wingless bird grew wings. He was still, however, the same goofy Moa I had grown to love.

"Wow! Look at me!" Moa flapped his new wings, rose a few feet, and dove headfirst into the grass. "Guess I need to practice."

"I guess." I grinned and went to sit with Queen Patchouli under a large willow. She was holding the baby again. "Asa didn't sleep very long."

"Babies sleep when they want," Queen Patchouli said. "And fairy babies develop faster than humans so they don't sleep as much. Would you like to hold her again?"

"Yes, thank you." I took the baby in my arms and stared into her big blue eyes. "You're so cute! I can't believe you'll be in charge of all this someday."

Asa giggled and cooed. Then, just like a human baby, she suddenly grabbed my pendant. "Trinee!"

I gasped. "Did she just say my name?"

"She's a fairy queen and very smart," Queen Patchouli said.

"And very special," I said with a yawn. Despite my power nap, I was having trouble keeping my eyes open.

Queen Patchouli took the baby, and I leaned back against the tree trunk. I glanced at the Ananya family talisman, knowing that, like my mother, I would wear it every day and night until the time came to pass it on again.

Only I wouldn't be passing on exactly the same necklace my mother had given me.

The greenstone beads and round pendant were laced with gold, a gift to me from a friend, the future Queen of all Aventurine.

The next time I opened my eyes, I saw my Maori kite. It was hanging on the wall with the wooden fishhook and the framed photo of Mom and me flying kites in New Zealand.

I was home.

Sunlight spilled through my window, and I could hear the faint sound of Dad's Sunday-morning television news shows.

It was my birthday. I was thirteen.

But more importantly, I was a fairy-godmother-in-training who had successfully completed her first mission in Aventurine.

I couldn't wait to tell Mom, but I was feeling a little too lazy to get up just yet. So much had happened in the fairy world I wanted to enjoy staying in bed a few minutes with absolutely nothing to do.

Except redecorate.

I sat up and looked around with a new perspective. The unimaginative, practically empty bedroom had been ideal for Trinity the mathematician, who hated clutter, liked order, and didn't believe magic was real.

It was way too stark and uninviting for the new me, and I started making changes in my head. First, I'd trade in my plain beige bedspread and window blinds for a comforter and curtains with a bright leaf and flower pattern. Then I'd paint the ceiling blue with white clouds.

I would never mess up my space with useless junk, but a few potted plants would look nice and add oxygen to the stuffy, indoor air. Kerka's friend Birdie at school had a green thumb that seemed magical. I was sure she'd have lots of tips and advice for a beginning apartment gardener.

On the other hand, I'd never change the three things that I had always cherished. The kite, fishhook, and picture above my desk reflected my life before I turned thirteen, and they were exactly where they should be. However, I wanted to add something that represented Aventurine and the person I'd become —

"Oh, no!" I looked down. I was wearing pajamas. The Ananya necklace was around my neck, but the harness and the back-pack were gone.

And so was Targa's exquisitely carved rose bead.

I couldn't believe the Curi-poo's gift had been left behind, and I began a frantic search. The wooden bead wasn't under the covers or on the floor beside the bed. I was trying hard not to shed tears and losing the battle. Then I saw it on my nightstand.

I didn't remember putting the bead by the velvet necklace box, but I decided not to question how the precious Curipoo thing had made it between worlds. It was mine to keep forever, and that's what mattered. I put the bead in the nightstand drawer for safekeeping until I found just the right display box.

I yawned again and slumped back against my pillows. Targa's bead was the only solid souvenir I had, but it wasn't the only thing I had brought back from the fairy world. My memories were vivid, and I wanted Zally to draw a poster-sized picture map of the tree. I was going to ask her tonight at my slumber party. I was sure she'd say yes, especially when I told her I wanted to frame and hang it on one of my way-too-bare walls.

Although I'd probably have to endure more than one "I told you so," I was anxious to tell my friends about my quest. Sumi would insist that spoongas are beautiful, and then she'd design an exotic cloud people dress. I wasn't sure Kerka would teach me the combat Kalis moves Queen Mangi had so elegantly executed, but I was prepared to beg.

Mostly, they'd all be glad they didn't have to

listen to any more logical arguments about why magic wasn't real.

"Are you up?" My mother opened the door and came in with a breakfast tray.

"Awake," I joked. "But not up yet."

"I thought you might be hungry for some brekkie." She set the tray on the nightstand.

"Thanks." I grinned when I saw the typical Kiwi breakfast she had prepared. "Bangers with pikelets! My favorite."

"You mean sausage and pancakes," Dad said as he passed the doorway. "That's American for bangers and pickles!" His voice echoed down the hall as he kept walking.

"Pikelets!" I yelled, laughing.

"Smothered in jam and whipped cream," Mom added.

"That's the only way!" I took a sip of orange juice and cut a small piece of pancake. I was full after eating so much at the naming ceremony, but Mom didn't know that. She didn't even know I had been to Aventurine.

"Did you sleep well?" She sat on the edge of the bed and gave me a quizzical look.

"Yes," I said. "When I wasn't climbing a giant tree or flying a kite to a cloud kingdom or rescuing the future Queen of Aventurine, I slept great."

"You went on a quest." Mom clasped her hands and smiled slowly. Then she frowned. "You rescued the *future* Queen of Aventurine?"

"Her name is Asa," I said. "It's a long story."

"I've got time." Mom pulled her legs up and nibbled a sausage while she listened.

I could tell she was busting with pride when I outlined my mission, but she frowned when I explained I had to save the baby from hostile people who tossed intruders off their cloud.

"It's hard to believe such horrid people live in Aventurine," Mom said, shaking her head.

"I know, and the mist people aren't the only ones," I said. "Hoon hates intruders and makes them walk the plank, and a fallen fairy called Kasandria kept birds locked up so they couldn't fly." My mother looked dismayed until I added, "But I learned to fly and freed all the birds, and most of the beings I met were wonderful."

She loved hearing about the Curipoo and wished she had met Moa.

"He was a hero," Mom said.

"Yes," I said. "He saved me and the baby."

Another flicker of disbelief flashed across Mom's face.

"What?" I asked.

"I'm sorry, Trinity, but"—Mom shrugged and

grinned—"it's just hard to imagine you with a baby. They're so messy, and you're so . . . so . . ."

"Neat?" I smiled, then gushed just like the queens. "But Asa is so adorable! Maybe not quite as adorable as the Curipoo, but almost. I wouldn't mind baby-sitting for her. She likes me."

Mom frowned again. "What happened to the Ananya talisman? It looks different."

I unhooked the necklace and put it in Mom's hand. "Asa touched it. The beads and pendant have gold in them now."

"That's powerful magic," Mom said.

"I'm sorry I didn't believe you," I said, "about magic being real."

"You do now," Mom said. "That's the important thing."

"But not the only important thing." I paused, wanting to ask but not certain I wanted an answer. I decided I had to know. "Will I still be able to fly?"

"I assume so, when you go back to Aventurine." Mom saw the disappointment on my face and gripped my knee. "You'll fly here, too, Trinity. Just not the same way. I got my wings when I became a pilot."

I was glad the human world still operated under absolute rules I understood, but that didn't make the loss of my flying power easier.

"I want wings, too, but—" I wasn't sure I should say what I was thinking. I was happy to have the Ananya necklace, but there was something else I wanted just for me.

"But?" Mom pressed me. "What do you want, Trinity?"

"I want a bird," I blurted out.

"Like a pet?" Mom asked.

"Like a friend I can keep in my room," I said. "A parrot, I think. They talk."

"I'll ask your father," Mom said as she stood up. "But don't worry. I'm sure he'll say yes."

"Thanks, Mom!" I jumped up and hugged her. "Can I go to the park?"

She looked surprised. "To do what?"

"Climb a tree?" I winced sheepishly, but Mom didn't make me feel silly for wanting to spend my first day as a teenager being a tomboy. She let me go.

I finished most of my breakfast and then changed into jeans, ankle boots, and a yellow scoop-neck tee. Then I grabbed my cell and raced for the front door.

My father looked up from the newspaper.

I paused, expecting the parental third degree: *Where are you going? Who are you going with? When will you be back?*

Dad didn't say anything. He just returned to his reading. Then, as I opened the door, he shouted, "Yes!"

Mom grinned from the sofa, gave me a thumbs-up, and flapped her hands like a bird. I could have my parrot!

I was so happy I practically floated out of the building.

The weather was warm and sunny, and I jogged all the way back to yesterday's picnic spot. It took no time at all to climb fifteen feet up the oak tree.

I sat in the crook of a branch and watched the people in the meadow. A few were flying kites. Most were playing ball, walking dogs, jogging, or sitting on blankets and benches reading newspapers and books. I had happily people-watched from the solitude of treetops for as long as I could remember, but now it seemed odd to be alone.

I had known Moa's absence would leave a hole in my life. I just hadn't realized how much I'd miss him, Sunset, and all the other birds.

Having a parrot wouldn't be quite the same, but it would help. I started thinking about names.

"Maybe Sunset the Second," I said out loud.

"What?" a voice asked from below.

I looked down. Parker was staring up with his hand shielding his eyes.

"What are you doing here?" I asked.

"Looking for you. I thought you might come back today to fly kites," Parker said. "What are you doing?"

"People-watching," I said.

"Want company?" Parker grabbed the lowest branch, but he didn't start climbing. He waited for my answer.

I liked Parker. He was cute and not an arrogant jerk. Besides, he had come to the park hoping to find me. That was three points in his favor.

Number four was the deciding one. My friends would believe everything that happened to me in Aventurine, but they'd never believe I had spent the afternoon with a boy.

I was glad my phone had a camera.

"Sure, Parker," I said. "Come on up."

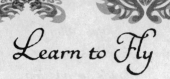

Learn to Fly

I'm not brave
Aren't you afraid too?
When the wind blew
I realized
It's just me and you

And a string
And a hole we just got to get through
In the sky
To learn to fly

It's not a trip to London, New York, or LA
It's the love that you pray for
The open door
It's your rich and your poor
It's the honesty play
It's the things that you say you want
Then try
To learn to fly

Come on come on come on
And open your arms wide
Out on the ledge
Up to the edge
Close your eyes tight
Feels like falling

Sky is calling
Earth is moving
Clouds are passing

Come on come on come on
And open your arms wide
Out on the ledge
Up to the edge
Close your eyes tight
It's the honesty play
Things that you say you want
Then try

Come on come on come on
And open your arms wide
Out on the ledge
Up to the edge
Close your eyes tight
Feels like falling
Sky is calling
Earth is moving
Clouds are passing
By

Come on come on
And learn to fly

Come on come on
And learn to fly

Acknowledgments

Learning to fly means taking chances and believing in yourself, especially when there is very little evidence that you'll make it. Many people in my life have helped me in difficult moments—the ones going up *and* the ones coming down. My father always believed in me, as did my brother and sister. My old friends Rob, LG, Laura, Mo, and Mary; my newer friends Ken and Chris; as well as my three sons, Shane, Evan, and Dustin, have helped me stay the course through every failure and redo. They encouraged me to be an Ananya Lineage girl, a totally unique individual. *Ananya* means "unique" in Sanskrit.

If you are "zigging" while everyone around you is "zagging," consider yourself an Ananya Lineage girl and embrace it. You are probably ahead of your time—a leader and a visionary. Go for it! Find your tribe, those people who will love you for who you really are.

About the Author

Jan Bozarth was raised in an international family in Texas in the sixties, the daughter of a Cuban mother and a Welsh father. She danced in a ballet company at eleven, started a dream journal at thirteen, joined a surf club at sixteen, studied flower essences at eighteen, and went on to study music, art, and poetry in college. As a girl, she dreamed of a life that would weave these different interests together. Her dream came true when she grew up and had a big family and a music and writing career. Jan is now a grandmother and writes stories and songs for young people. She often works with her own grown-up children, who are musicians and artists in Austin, Texas. (Sometimes Jan is even the fairy godmother who encourages them to believe in their dreams!) Jan credits her own mother, Dora, with handing down her wisdom: Dream big and never give up.

Dhara's Book

Coming soon!

Meet Dhara—she refuses to believe she is an orphan and knows that if she can just find her way to Aventurine, she'll finally be able to rescue her parents.

Have you read the first
Fairy Godmother Academy book?

Birdie's
Book

Will Kerka learn the right Kalis moves
in time to save her sisters?
Find out in

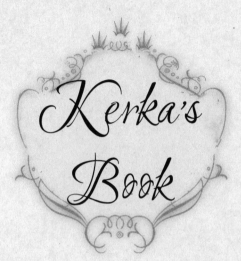

Kerka's
Book

Will Zally's ability to talk with animals
be enough to save a fairy queen?
Find out in

Zally's Book

Will Lilu's talent for weaving the elements
be enough to stop a magical hurricane?
Find out in

Lilu's
Book

Will Sumi's shape-shifting ability help her
defeat an evil fairy queen?
Find out in

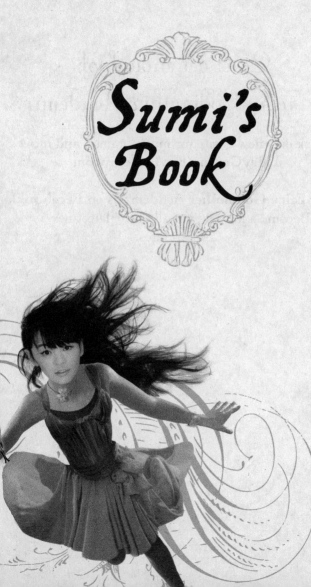

Sumi's
Book

Can't get enough of
the Fairy Godmother Academy?

Check out the website for music, games, and more!
FairyGodmotherAcademy.com

The Fairy Godmother Academy is on Facebook!
Become a fan and get all of the latest news
and updates.